If Sop... ...ng deal of being close to him, she'd only succeed in allowing him to see...well, that this was a big deal to her.

He wrapped his arms around her waist, picked her up and twirled her around in a circle. "What was it you said?" Michael's chocolaty eyes lit. "That my parents would be dancing-a-jig happy?"

"I knew they'd be pleased." Sophia hoped the breathlessness she heard in her words was a figment of her freaked-out imagination.

"If you hadn't spoken up," he whispered, "I don't know how long I'd have waited to tell them they had a granddaughter."

"I can see that." She sighed, swiftly getting caught up in the vortex that seemed to spin crazily around them.

"I want you to know how grateful I am."

She was going to utter his name sharply. She was going to plant her hand on his chest. She was going to lean away from him.

But she did none of those things.

Dear Reader,

This month seems to be all about change. Just as our heroines are about to have some fabulous makeovers, Silhouette Romance will be undergoing some changes over the next months that we believe will make this classic line even more relevant to your challenging lives. Of course, you'll still find some of your favorite SR authors and favorite themes, but look for some new names, more international settings and even more emotional reads.

Over the next few months the company is also focusing attention on the new direction and package for Harlequin Romance. We believe that the blend of authors and stories coming in that line will thrill readers and satisfy every emotion.

Just like our heroines, my responsibilities will be changing, as I will be working on Harlequin NEXT. Please know how much I have enjoyed sharing these heartwarming, aspirational reads with you.

With all best wishes,

Ann Leslie Tuttle
Associate Senior Editor

Please address questions and book requests to:
Silhouette Reader Service
U.S.: 3010 Walden Ave., P.O. Box 1325, Buffalo, NY 14269
Canadian: P.O. Box 609, Fort Erie, Ont. L2A 5X3

Nanny
and the Beast

DONNA CLAYTON

SILHOUETTE *Romance*®
Published by Silhouette Books
America's Publisher of Contemporary Romance

For Joy with love

To Dad
You have shown me the meaning of joyful and
wholehearted dedication to God and family;
You have fostered my faith; And you continue to
teach me, by flawless example, how to be a loving
and supportive parent.
Thank you.

SILHOUETTE BOOKS

ISBN-13: 978-0-373-19828-3
ISBN-10:   0-373-19828-0

NANNY AND THE BEAST

Copyright © 2006 by Donna Fasano

This edition published by arrangement with Harlequin Books S.A.

Visit Silhouette Books at www.eHarlequin.com

Printed in U.S.A.

Books by Donna Clayton

Silhouette Romance

Mountain Laurel #720
Taking Love in Stride #781
Return of the Runaway Bride #999
Wife for a While #1039
Nanny and the Professor #1066
Fortune's Bride #1118
Daddy Down the Aisle #1162
**Miss Maxwell Becomes
    a Mom* #1211
*Nanny in the Nick of Time #1217
**Beauty and the Bachelor
    Dad* #1223
*†The Stand-By Significant
    Other* #1284
*†Who's the Father of Jenny's
    Baby?* #1302
The Boss and the Beauty #1342
His Ten-Year-Old Secret #1373

Her Dream Come True #1399
Adopted Dad #1417
His Wild Young Bride #1441
**The Nanny Proposal #1477
***The Doctor's Medicine
    Woman* #1483
**Rachel and the M.D. #1489
Who Will Father My Baby? #1507
In Pursuit of a Princess #1582
*††The Sheriff's 6-Year-Old
    Secret* #1623
*††The Doctor's Pregnant
    Proposal* #1635
††Thunder in the Night #1647
The Nanny's Plan #1701
Because of Baby #1723
Bound by Honor #1797
Nanny and the Beast #1828

Silhouette Books

The Coltons
Close Proximity

Logan's Legacy
Royal Seduction

*The Single Daddy Club
†Mother & Child
**Single Doctor Dads
††The Thunder Clan

DONNA CLAYTON

is a bestselling, award-winning author. She and her husband divide their time between homes in northern Delaware and Maryland's Eastern Shore. They have two sons. Donna also writes women's fiction as Donna Fasano.

Please write to Donna care of Silhouette Books. She'd love to hear from you!

Dear Reader,

Nannies (and stories featuring nannies) have always held a place near and dear to my heart. You see, my sister-in-law, Joy, trained and worked as a nanny. From her, I learned that the amazing women (and, I'm sure, a few men) who choose to become nannies have a special love for and devotion to children.

Joy was born and raised in a small town in Kansas. She left Lebo to attend nanny school and earned her certification. Joy then moved to Washington, D.C., where she lived with and worked for a family with two children. She loved her job and was dedicated to those children. After a few years, she met my brother and is currently experiencing her very own "happily ever after."

Joy's experience as a nanny prepared her to become the most nurturing of mothers. Her children are loving and mannerly and kind and smart as can be! She's done an amazing job of raising them, and I hope she knows how very proud I am of the job she has done. I also hope she knows how much I love her and that I'm happy to call her sister. (Thanks for answering all my nanny questions, Joy!)

I hope all of you enjoy reading Sophia's story as much as I enjoyed writing it!

All the best,

Donna Clayton

Chapter One

"It's him! It's *him!* He just pulled up out front."

Sophia Stanton refused to let the tension in Karen's voice rattle her. Her part-time assistant was easily flustered.

"Him?" Sophia asked, placing her pen on the desktop and glancing toward the doorway. "*Him* who?"

Karen's eyes widened and her voice lowered to a whisper. "The Beast." She reached up and plucked at the short, spiky locks behind her ear. Then she craned her neck to look out the front window. "He just took his baby out of the back of his SUV." She sucked in a tight breath. "And Lily just got out, too. Her face is four shades of red."

Sophia stifled a groan. She didn't need more aggravation this morning; two of her girls had called in sick and replacements were yet to be found. But knowing the track record of Mr. Michael Taylor, aka "The Beast," she steeled herself for the worst.

When it came to providing care for his month-old daughter, the man seemed impossible to please. He'd fired two of Sophia's nannies in the past three weeks. The young women had come back to the office reporting that he was demanding and inflexible, so much so that everyone at The Nanny Place was certain he must sport horns and a spiked tail. One thing was certain—Mr. Taylor was fast becoming a beastly pain in Sophia's butt.

"Okay," Sophia told Karen, inhaling deeply to prepare herself. "Let's just stay calm. Keep Lily out there with you, and show him in here immediately. And then I need for you to get in touch with Terry. Ask her if she's able to cover for Isabel today."

"Terry lives below the canal," Karen reminded her. "She'll never reach the city in time for Mrs. Schaffer to get to work on time."

"I'll call and explain." Sophia gathered up the paperwork on her desk and set it to one side. The Beast would be here any second. "And I'll find someone to fill in for Paula, too. Just as soon as I take care of this problem."

Karen tugged at her hair again, the pen curled between her fingers nearly poking her chin. "They're here." Trepidation rippled through her whisper. "Good luck," she added, before disappearing from the doorway.

Sophia stood, smoothed her hand over the skirt of her dark suit and then paused long enough to take one more deep breath, the kind she'd learned in her yoga class. Her instructor swore yoga could help in every aspect of her life and right now she was willing to take all the help she could get.

Michael Taylor didn't just walk in to her office, he stormed in, closing the door firmly behind him. Anger honed his handsome features and seemed out of sync with the awkward gentleness with which he cradled his baby girl.

His most striking feature was his gaze. Those deep brown eyes flashed with extreme intensity—irritation, yes, but something else, too, some powerful force emanating from within. He had the kind of good looks and trim, athletic body that made a sensible woman think thoughts she shouldn't, and consider doing things she normally wouldn't. Sophia wouldn't have been the least surprised to learn that females who passed him on the street routinely broke out into appreciative wolf whistles.

"Good morning, Mr. Taylor," Sophia greeted, infusing a bright friendliness into her voice while completely ignoring the palpable ire radiating off the man.

"There's not much good about it, I'm afraid." Annoyance sharpened every word.

Oh, yeah, women might whistle for his attention, but all they'd get for their trouble was a rumbling growl.

"I fired Lily this morning," he told her.

Sophia wanted to swear, but held her tongue. He was a client and she had to do her best to please him. Her mind raced. Did she even have anyone else willing to work for the man?

"We need to fix the problem I've been having with the nannies you're sending me, Ms. Stanton, and we need to fix it now."

A sigh of frustration gathered in Sophia's chest, but she didn't allow it to escape with any kind of real force. "Of course we do. And we will, I assure you." Then she asked, "What did Lily do?"

"It's what she didn't do. She didn't follow the rules. It's not as if my needs are difficult to meet. But I do insist that any nanny working for me will follow the damn rules."

The Damn Rules was an apt description, Sophia thought. Apparently, there were literally pages of them, and they covered every conceivable notion when it came to his daughter's care. There was even a dress code for the nannies. It wasn't enough that the young women she'd sent him were highly trained in childcare. Michael Taylor wanted them to look and dress and act a certain way. To better focus on the childcare, is what she'd heard. Demanding such a thing was his prerogative, she guessed. However, no woman wanted to be told she couldn't wear nail polish or eye shadow or dangly earrings, or that her skirt had to hang below her knees, or that her hair had to be pulled back in a bun. A bun! Buns went out with pixie bobs, for goodness sake. What was he running? A Catholic grade school? It was ridiculous.

"First off," he continued, "I take exception to the fact that the nannies you're sending me are barely out of their teens. How can *girls*—" the emphasis he placed on the word made Sophia want to cringe "—with so little life experience make sound, common-sense judgments in day-to-day circumstances, let alone emergency situations? I'm supposed to trust them with my daughter?"

"I beg your pardon, Mr. Taylor." Although she understood his fears—he *was* a new father—she felt she had to stand up for her employees. "Both of them—" Lily flashed into Sophia's mind, and she instantly corrected herself. "All three of the nannies you've fired this month have been thoroughly trained. They have earned a childcare diploma from an accredited nanny school as well as a medical safety certificate. That's the only way they qualify to register at The Nanny Place. I complete the background checks myself. Your daughter has been in capable hands—"

"I manage people for a living," he interrupted. "I have seen, firsthand, that training isn't always enough. A healthy dose of life experience goes a long way in helping people make sensible decisions when they're faced with even the most mundane choices. I'll take a forty-year-old with firm common sense over a green Gen-Xer any day of the week. The girls you've sent me need just that—a healthy dose of life experience. I don't want them acquiring it at the sake of Hailey's well-being."

"But—"

"No," he interrupted. "No buts. I want you to send me someone older. Someone wiser. Lily has worked for me for three days. She knows the daily schedule we keep. Yet she stepped into the shower just five minutes before I was supposed to leave for work. I want you to send me someone who can follow a simple schedule."

Sophia silently groaned. Lily was going to get an earful from her.

"I want someone with professionalism," he continued, "and experience. Someone who's lived long enough to have gained some practical knowledge of what it takes to care for an infant. A motherly type. Better yet, a grandmotherly type."

"Sounds like you want a Mrs. Doubtfire." The joking sarcasm rolled off her tongue before she'd had a chance to stop it.

He went dead silent for a moment, staring at her. Then the harsh angles of his face softened and he chuckled. He actually laughed. The sexy, delicious rumble was completely unexpected. Some sort of strange electricity shot through her body, scrambling her thoughts. This was a side of The Beast she'd never experienced. She blinked a couple of times in quick succession, and then gathered her wits as quickly as she could. Fostering the light-hearted moment seemed a good idea.

"Um, Mr. Taylor, you do know that, although she was great with children, she was a middle-aged man in drag? A fictional character created by some Hollywood screenwriter."

"Of course, I do."

His amusement was gone as quickly as it had come. But the humming current he'd cause to flutter through her lingered with irritating tenacity.

"I think I've made my needs quite clear," he told her. "If you're unable to provide what I'm asking, then that can only mean that your business motto is a sham. I don't mind telling you that I'm not happy, and I seriously think we ought to consider parting ways. I'll have to find a nanny on my own."

"Hold on just a second," Sophia said. Her mind raced. "Backing out of our contract is a little extreme, isn't it?"

She'd read that a satisfied customer might express his or her opinion about a company to approximately fifty friends, relatives and casual acquaintances, whereas a disgruntled one could be expected to complain to many times that.

"I don't think so. You've had three chances to send a nanny that would meet my approval. You've failed three times."

He sure didn't have a problem speaking his mind, now, did he?

She hadn't faced this kind of fiasco since opening the doors of The Nanny Place. No one had ever called her a failure before. To the contrary, *Delaware Today* magazine had awarded her business the title of "Best childcare in the city of Wilmington" for the last two years running.

"What you don't seem to understand," Sophia stressed, putting every effort into coming up with a swift recovery, "is that when women reach that 'older, wiser' stage you've described, they're either ready to settle down and have children of their own—"

She shook her head, unable to believe the words tumbling out of her mouth. They had a jarring, sexist ring to them, but that couldn't be helped. She needed an argument. *Any* argument.

"Or they're ready to retire, do some traveling, take a cruise, enjoy their golden years. *Or* their own grandchildren. I only have two women over the age of twenty-five registered at The Nanny Place. Both are grandmothers in their mid-to-late fifties and they're on long-term assignments with families in Wilmington."

He glanced down at his sleeping daughter, and then leveled his gaze at Sophia. Calmly, he said, "So you're telling me the bottom line is I'm going to remain an unsatisfied client?"

Discontent crackled in the air as he waited for her response and Sophia fought the urge to squirm. Damn it! The man wasn't going to best her.

"I intend to make sure you are *very* satisfied, Mr. Taylor," she blurted out. Heat suffused her face when she realized what she'd said and how those words could very easily be misconstrued. Ignoring the embarrassment she felt, she plowed full steam ahead. "Even if I'm the one who has to come do the job," she heard herself say.

His brows arched the slightest bit and he absently smoothed his fingers down the short length of his daughter's milky arm. "Now there's a good idea." He nodded slowly, evidently liking the notion more with each passing second.

Her comment had been merely meant to assure him she honestly intended to find him the perfect nanny, and she wouldn't stop trying until she'd succeeded. Apparently, he hadn't taken it that way. Not at all. A sense of panic washed over her. "Mr. Taylor—"

"You're certainly older than twenty-five," he mused, his fingers toying with the edge of the baby blanket.

She bristled. He made her sound downright matronly.

"And the fact that you're running your own business tells me that you've got intellect and common sense. Two important characteristics for the person I want caring for my daughter."

He was clearly warming up to this surprising turn of events. She opened her mouth to speak.

"If you spend a few weeks getting to know Hailey," he said, not giving her a chance to restate what she'd actually intended, "getting to know me, getting to know our situation and our needs, you'd be better equipped to find the kind of nanny I'm looking for."

It was on the tip of her tongue to say "but…but," to backpedal herself out of the tight space she'd inadvertently talked herself into. She couldn't do this! She had a business to run. She wasn't a nanny. She was the administrator.

Oh, she'd had all the proper training and she even took over childcare duties once in a while when the rare problem or an emergency cropped up, so she was fully capable of—

"I usually take dead silence to have negative meaning," he said, studying her intently. "Should I assume you aren't going to honor your guarantee? And that your motto of 'no client left unsatisfied' is simply a string of meaningless words?" He lifted a shoulder. "If that's the case, then I have no choice but to cancel our contract as of this moment."

"Wait. I'm not saying any of that," she sputtered. "I'm also not saying I won't do it. I'm just thinking things through. Working out the logistics."

Her mind whirled; other than scheduling appointments with prospective clients and handling a few glitches that arose, there wasn't a whole lot Sophia couldn't take care of with her cell phone. And her assistant, Karen, had been asking—no, *begging*—to go full-time since coming to work for her, but up until now Sophia had only needed help in the office during the busy morning hours.

"I hope you're thinking fast," he persisted, "because I don't have all day." He tenderly shifted his daughter to his other arm and checked his watch. "In fact, I have to be at the office in forty-five minutes."

Darn! He wasn't going to give her an inch. She gritted her teeth. All he was worried about was himself. What about *her* business? What about the people depending on *her?*

But how else was she going to make Michael Taylor happy, at this point, other than to take over as his daughter's nanny for the few weeks, as he was demanding?

Keeping him happy would mean keeping her pristine business reputation. That was very important to her. She prided herself on the fact that not one client, past or present, had a single grievance against her or The Nanny Place. Oh, there were small insignificant matters that surfaced from time to time between the nannies and their employers, but there hadn't been even one instance where Sophia hadn't been able to straighten everything out, and make everyone concerned content and happy. She refused to allow this man to mar her perfect record.

"Okay," she said. "I'll do it. If you'll let me sort a few things out here, I can be at your place in forty-five minutes."

"Excellent. Less than forty-five minutes, actually. I'll head home and wait for you." He turned toward the door.

"Hold it," she said, an idea popping into her head. "Why don't you just leave Hailey with me now? I can use your carseat to get her back to your place. That way you won't be late for work, and I can take my time getting things settled here."

Seemed like a perfectly good plan to her, but evidently he didn't think so.

"Won't work." His tone brooked no argument. "We still have to go over the rules and Hailey's schedule. They're at my place. Typed out in black and white. I'd also feel more comfortable if I had the chance to show you around. Make you acquainted with where things are."

That did make sense, she thought.

"You have my address?" he asked.

"Yes, of course." She hurried around him and opened the door. This was happening much too fast. She followed him out to the reception area where she noticed that Lily stood stewing near Karen's desk. Her hair was still damp from that ill-fated shower she'd taken this morning. Karen looked as if she expected something horrible to happen at any moment. Sophia quickly added, "I'll have my assistant download driving directions to your home from the 'Net, Mr. Taylor. No problem."

As soon as Sophia spoke the words, Karen's head dipped and her fingers flew over her computer keyboard.

His back was to Sophia as he walked across the room and headed for the door. His pin-striped dress shirt accentuated his broad shoulders, and his navy trousers cuddled a firm butt. He paused and turned to face Sophia, and her gaze darted up to where it belonged—his face.

Again, he checked his watch. "I'll see you soon, Ms. Stanton."

She nodded once, and then he was out the door. She continued to stare as he stepped off the curb, her gaze inadvertently traveling down the full length of him.

Her spine straightened and she blinked. She was going to have to hustle to get everything done here at the office. She made a quick mental list; a short talk with Lily, then give Karen instructions, a couple of phone calls, a quick stop in the powder room and she'd be out the door.

"Lily said he fired her." Karen's eyes were wide.

"It was so unfair," Lily chimed in.

Karen shifted in her chair. "Who are you going to send this time, Sophia? Do we have anyone left who isn't afraid of that guy?"

"We most certainly do," Sophia murmured, her gaze continuing to linger on Michael Taylor. The morning sunlight burnished his tawny hair. Why she was standing here wasting time baffled her, yet there was something about the man that made it hard to tear her eyes away.

"Well, *who?*"

Ignoring her assistant's question, Sophia turned her attention to Lily. "What happened this morning? How could you get yourself fired after only three days?"

Lily's chin tipped upward.

Sophia lifted her hands in frustration. "He said you showered late. That you couldn't keep to the schedule."

"This had nothing to do with his precious schedule," Lily spat out. "This was about that stupid robe rule. I wasn't wearing mine this morning."

"He has a rule about wearing a robe?" Karen asked. "That's a new one, isn't it?"

"He added it the second day I worked for him. He has rules for *everything*," Lily complained. "Rules for when his daughter eats, when she sleeps. What music is played in the house. What books are read and when. There are pages and pages of rules. And he keeps adding to them."

Sophia had heard it all before from the other nannies who had cared for Michael Taylor's daughter.

"And the ones dictating our dress code are the worst. I wanted to flip on the bitch-switch several times, Sophia. But I controlled myself." Lily turned her eyes to Karen. "And even though it cost me that job, I refused to say I was sorry this morning. Heck, I was just being me."

Obvious rebellion tinged Lily's voice. Sophia crossed her arms. "And what exactly does that mean?"

Sucking in a long-suffering breath, Lily explained, "The baby had been up most of last night. I knew she wasn't going to wake up anytime soon. I needed a shower so I could feel human, okay? I was tired. I forgot my robe. Why should it matter, anyway, when my room was right across the hall from the bathroom?"

Sophia's patience thinned. "Okay, so you weren't wearing a robe. What *were* you wearing?"

There was mutiny in Lily's silence.

Karen softly sang, "Can you say scanty panties from Victoria's Secret?"

Picturing the barely clad models in the famous lingerie catalog, astonishment made Sophia's jaw go slack. "Lily! You didn't. How could you? Why *would* you? You know he's asked all the nannies to be covered from neck to knee. Why would you prance around half-naked in front of the man?"

Lily pursed her lips, her expression a mixture of anger and insult. "I wasn't prancing. And I was wearing a nightie." Then she muttered, "The least he could have done was notice. I swear the man has ice water running through his veins."

Only a nineteen-year-old would feel offended when her employer hadn't seemed to notice her shapely figure even though he'd specifically asked not to see it.

"So you did it on purpose." Sophia let her hands fall to her sides.

"Of course I didn't do it on purpose," Lily said. "I told you. I'd been up half the night with Hailey. I was exhausted. What I wear to bed is my business."

Sophia rubbed at the dull ache thumping behind her temple. "Being caught in the hallway wearing skimpy pj's shouldn't warrant being fired."

Chagrin made Lily balk. "It wasn't the first time." She grimaced, reluctantly admitting, "Or the second."

Karen snickered, and Sophia silenced her with a sharp glance. She'd heard enough of Lily's predicament.

"What you're saying is that he had good reason for implementing a robe rule." Remembering the ticking clock, Sophia's irritation simmered over. "I don't have time for this. Lily, if you can't be more considerate of the people paying your salary, maybe you don't deserve to work here."

"But I need this job!"

"I know you do. That's why I'm not letting you go. But I am putting you on probation. If you show me you've learned something from this experience—"

"Yeah." Karen smirked. "Like maybe buying some flannel nightgowns and white cotton granny panties."

"Hush, Karen." Sophia had had all she could take.

She looked at Lily. "You can fill in for Paula for today and Karen will work on getting you another full-time position."

"I will?" Karen asked, clearly surprised. "But that's not usually in my job description."

"Your job description is changing as of right now." The wake Sophia created as she breezed past Karen's desk on her way to the powder room made several papers flutter. "You've been asking to go full-time, haven't you?"

"You know I have." Karen went very still and serious.

Sophia flipped on the powder room light. "Well, now's your chance. You'll be running the office for the next two weeks. It's a big job. Can you handle the responsibility?" She glanced into the mirror over the sink.

Gathering her thick hair in her fingers, Sophia twisted it into a knot and secured it with a clip. She knew Mr. Taylor liked his nannies to keep their hair out of their eyes.

"Are you kidding me? You know I can handle it. That reminds me, Terry's on her way to the Schaffers to cover for Isabel. I've already called Mrs. Schaffer to let her know Terry would be late. But what's going on? Where will you be?"

"Yeah, Sophia," Lily chimed in. "You going to tell us what's up? You never said which lucky nanny gets to go work for The Beast."

While Lily talked, Sophia turned on the faucet and scrubbed the makeup from her face. Then she patted her forehead, cheeks and chin dry. "He likes his nannies plain, right?"

Slowly but surely, both Karen and Lily figured out the plan. "*You?*" they asked in unison.

"That's right." Sophia smoothed her hand over the lapel of her jacket and then tugged at its hem. "I'm saving the spotless reputation of The Nanny Place. If Mr. Michael Taylor wants a sedate, older nanny, I'm going to give him just that," she declared, adjusting her Mrs. Doubtfire bun.

"But you've never gone out on an assignment for more than a couple hours, a day at most. Why would you—"

"Because he's left me no choice, Karen. That man fired three perfectly acceptable nannies."

"Damn right, he did," Lily grumbled.

Karen smirked. "Lily, you might be perfectly qualified to take care of a baby, but I have to point out that you *did* break the robe rule."

Lily made a face at Karen.

Sophia ignored the ruckus. "I need to get over there myself and see exactly what the problem is. Obviously, there's something going on with that man. I need to figure this out before I start losing clients." She absently fingered the buttons at each cuff. "I just have to remember my ultimate goal."

"You have a goal?" Karen asked.

"Oh, yes. I've got two actually." A slow smile spread across her lips and she forced her tense shoulder muscles to relax. "I'm going to preserve my pristine business reputation by making Michael Taylor happy."

The mischievous sparkle in Sophia's eyes had Lily prompting, "Yes? *And?*"

There was determination in every syllable when Sophia declared, "Whatever it takes, I'm going to tame the flippin' Beast."

Chapter Two

The Palisades condominiums were *the* place to live in Wilmington. The great slabs of white Carrara marble that encased the twenty-five-story building glistened in the morning sun. Bands of glossy black stone shot skyward at each corner, the sharp angles of the architecture imparting a distinctly contemporary feel. Sophia had heard real estate commercials for the condos on the radio. The extensive complex boasted both indoor and outdoor swimming pools, various sports courts, several workout facilities and a professionally landscaped walking path, not to mention the two-, three- and four-bedroom luxury residences that were available. The place was a lush oasis smack in the middle of the bustling city.

Sophia parked her car, got out and squinted up at the tall building, knowing she'd never earn the kind of money it took to buy a home in this *au courant* high-rise.

The lofty ceiling of the lobby was crowned with a huge abstract light fixture made of individual swirls of gem-hued blown glass, a gorgeous splash of vibrant color against the otherwise stark black-and-white surroundings.

The elevator doors slid open on a whisper. Sophia stepped out into the hallway of the top floor, and when the doors closed behind her, the soft jazz she'd enjoyed during the swift, short ride was silenced. The well-lit corridor had been painted a tasteful shade of taupe. Conceptualistic paintings hung at regular intervals on the walls, and with each step she took, Sophia's heels sunk into the plush henna-colored carpet. There wasn't a single detail here that wasn't impressively lavish. She stopped in front of the solid mahogany door of Michael Taylor's condo and pressed the buzzer.

He pulled open the door, and immediately she was once again struck by the simmering intensity he exuded.

"Right on time," he observed, approval brightening his tone. "Did you remember to bring proof of your childcare credentials? I assumed you were qualified when I was at your office, but I'd still like to see the paperwork."

Evidently, he wasn't one to waste time with amiable greetings, but rather got right down to the business at hand. Somehow, that didn't surprise her.

"Of course. Everything you need is right here." Stepping into the foyer, she handed him the manila envelope filled with the usual information her nannies supplied to their employers—a resume complete with education history and work experience, proof of a recent physical, a copy of her current driving record and child-care and emergency safety accreditation.

He was so serious when he took the envelope from her that she could easily see how the young women she'd sent to care for his daughter might be intimidated. Would it hurt the man to smile?

She knew he had it in him. She'd heard him laugh this morning, and the memory alone was enough to make the hairs on her arms stand on end even now. Unwittingly, she smoothed her palms over her upper arms.

The scent of his cologne enveloped her, and she found the warm, woodsy fragrance more than a little pleasing.

No matter how severe his persona, though, she was still amazed by that purring undercurrent of energy radiating from him, around him—around *them*. It was the same force she'd felt when he was in her office, and it plucked at her with the same dogged insistence now as it had then.

As he looked over her information, Sophia attempted to ignore the invisible static by checking out his home. From where she stood, she could see into the living room to the left, and a bit of the kitchen to the right. The black leather and rich coppery metals in the living room were warm and masculine. All she could see of the kitchen were cabinets made of a deep red cherry wood and bit of black granite countertop.

"Everything looks adequate." He glanced up from the papers he'd been studying. "Let's go inside where we can talk."

Adequate? A smile tickled her lips, but she quelled it as she followed him into the living room. She'd graduated from university with top honors and a double major in child development and business. She'd started her company fresh out of college and had nearly exhausted herself working full-time during the days to establish The Nanny Place, while earning her Delaware child-care certificate in the evenings just for emergencies

like this one when she had to step in and take over at
the grassroots level. She would describe herself as a
confident, successful businesswoman, educated in both
the physical and emotional aspects of childrearing. And
he thought her credentials only adequate. Sophia
wondered what a woman would have to do to impress
the man.

"On the coffee table there," he said, "is a detailed
inventory of what I expect."

Ah, Sophia thought, as she picked up the list with
interest and eased herself down onto the couch. So these
were the infamous rules. Just as Lily and the other fired
nannies had described, there were pages of them.

"Hailey fell asleep on the ride back home so I put her
back in her crib. She hasn't had her bath or her breakfast." He paced to the chair and sat down. "The schedule
for today is completely shot. Again."

"Well, maybe it's a good thing that the baby's having
a morning nap." Sophia kept her tone casual, hoping to
ease his irritation. "I talked with Lily after you left and
she said that Hailey was awake most of the night."

His handsome face went tight. "She wouldn't be up
in the night if the nannies would just do as I instruct
them. Keeping to the schedule is everything."

Sophia's first instinct was to defend the young women
who had come here to care for Hailey, to let him know
that schedules and babies didn't always mesh well, but
she bit her tongue. Arguing with him about his rigid
expectations before she'd had time to assess the rules—
to assess *him*—wasn't a good idea. She needed time to
take it all in and then she would worry about arguing.

Her best course of action, she decided, was to refrain
from kick-starting any antagonism between them.

Instead, she needed to remain calm and professional so she could become familiar with the situation. Smoothing his ruffled feathers should be priority number one, she reasoned silently. Surely his daughter would awaken soon and babies were notorious for sensing the stresses and anxieties in others. Sophia didn't need a fussy infant on her hands at the same time she was dealing with Michael.

"And that's all I ask you to do," he continued. "Follow the rules. They're simple enough. Keep to the schedule. How hard can that be?"

Apparently, he was still agitated from his confrontation with Lily and the need for having to drive to The Nanny Place.

"I understand that you're annoyed that you had to fire Lily this morning. Especially since you warned her about walking around in her nightgown—"

"I wouldn't call what she was wearing a nightgown. Short, lacy and completely transparent."

"*What?*" Sophia couldn't believe her ears.

"The girl was nearly naked."

Sophia's jaw went slack. "You're kidding?"

"I'm not," he said. "And if you're looking for the whole truth of the matter, it wasn't an accident."

"But she said—"

His square jaw dipped low. "Trust me on this. She wanted me to see her body, and she left nothing to the imagination."

Sophia frowned and murmured an apology on Lily's behalf. That girl was in for it, that was for certain.

He shrugged. "Young people act rashly. They don't think about consequences. I see it every day."

No wonder he'd stormed into her office like a roaring lion. In this day and age of sexual harassment in the workplace, he'd had every right to be furious. Heck, he'd had every right to fire her.

Sophia told him, "That should never have happened."

Awkwardness tightened the air. Finally, she said, "I promise you that I'll do everything in my power while I'm here to follow your guidelines to the letter."

As she made the pledge, she knew she was clinging to the age-old business adage that the client was always right. She was determined to do whatever it took to save her good business reputation. However, if she discovered that his rules were really as restrictive as she'd heard, she had every intention of somehow turning things around, of making him see that his agenda was way too rigid for the mere mortals who were caring for Hailey, not to mention a one-month-old infant.

"I appreciate that," he told her. But his tension didn't seem to lessen.

"I want you to know," he continued, "that your only job is to care for Hailey. I don't want you doing any housework or cooking or anything else while you're here. Your focus should be on my daughter."

That was a relief. One of the biggest complaints she heard from the nannies she placed was that parents kept adding responsibilities that had nothing whatsoever to do with childcare; running errands, performing household chores and such. One nanny was asked to attend a parent teacher conference at her charge's school. The young woman had felt awkward about approaching the parents, so Sophia had stepped in and clearly outlined everyone's proper role in the business relationship.

He went quiet for a moment, and Sophia finally had a chance to glance over the schedule he'd prepared.

"Were you in the military?" she asked, her eyebrows

arching a fraction. She really had been aiming to play it cool and not cause problems, but she reacted before she could stop herself.

Her question seemed to confuse him, so she explained. "The schedule you've set for Hailey is so…regimented. Up by seven, fed by seven-thirty, bathed and dressed by eight. Diaper change at nine, another at ten. Snack at ten thirty. Diaper change at eleven."

She peered at him over the top edge of the paper. "What if she isn't hungry at seven-thirty? Or what if she doesn't need a diaper change at ten?"

His jaw went taut. "What is it with you people?" he asked, exasperation sharpening his tone. "Whose child *is* this? How I want to parent my child is up to me, isn't it? You just finished promising me that you'd follow the guidelines."

"Yes, but I never said I wouldn't question the logic in them." Instantly, she realized that had been the wrong thing to say. "Look—" she held up her hand in an attempt to appease him "—all I'm saying is that—"

"I've already told you that I believe scheduling is everything," he interrupted. "She has to learn that meals are served at regular intervals. How else is she supposed to understand the program? How else is my daughter going to learn to fit in to my life?"

"Fit in to *your* life?" Did he not understand how outrageous his thinking was? "We're talking about a baby. Not a puppy. Hailey's brand-new to this world. She hasn't a clue about rules and schedules. As her father, you have to figure out what *Hailey's* schedule is. And although you may not like it, you have to arrange your life around her for a while. New parents are always complaining about feeling exhausted and overwhelmed, but—" she shrugged "—them's the breaks. You have to suck it up and live by Hailey's rules. Not vice versa."

She pointed to the rule regarding diaper changes. "You must be wasting an awful lot of disposable diapers. Hailey can't possibly need changing every hour."

"I would think that diaper rash is painful, and I would also think the best way to prevent it is to keep her bottom dry." He was positively glowering. Clearly, he was not a man who was used to explaining his actions or his motives.

Her gaze darted for an instant to his lips. He had a nice mouth, even when it formed a straight, hard line. When he'd laughed in her office earlier his whole face had changed. His expression relaxed. The muscles of his smooth shaven jaw had contracted and his lips had curled into a smile. A nice smile, she remembered, trying to hold on to the image.

"And besides that," he continued through gritted teeth, "at some time in the future my daughter has to realize she shouldn't be wetting her diaper. If her diaper is changed often enough, she might catch on to the concept more quickly."

The very idea tickled Sophia, and she let out a chuckle. It was only a small one, and she choked it off quickly, but her reaction only heightened his irritation; she could tell by the ire that flashed in his dark eyes.

She reigned herself in automatically, shaking her head as she said, "I'm sorry. I shouldn't laugh. I understand that this is a serious matter."

Even as she said the words, she had to fight back the humor bubbling up in her chest. Either he didn't know a thing about babies, or he was one of those overly diligent parents who pushed their children to the brink to achieve.

The thought of anyone thinking they could potty train a newborn, though, was downright silly to her.

"Forgive me," she said, luckily able to keep a straight face, "but I have to let you in on a little secret. It'll be many months—a couple of years even—before Hailey is ready to 'catch on' to the concept of potty training. And changing a dry diaper is like tossing money out the window."

Michael couldn't believe his ears…or his eyes. *This woman was laughing* at him. She attempted to hold it back, but humor was dancing in her deep, blue eyes. Not only that, but she'd questioned the schedule he'd put so much thought and effort into. She wouldn't rest until she'd criticized each and every rule, too, he was certain.

Had she just told him to *suck it up?* Had she really just suggested that he let his one month old daughter make her own rules? What kind of craziness was that?

"If you're not worried about the money," Sophia continued, "think of the environment. It's one thing to throw soiled diapers into a landfill, but perfectly clean ones? Come on. That's harmful for the world and everyone in it."

Her gaze continued to twinkle. She was obviously a people person; someone who attempted to chastise gently and without insult. A person who had been trained to work with children.

Well, he was no child.

He wasn't offended by anything she'd said, but he did feel like a total idiot. Would it really be years before Hailey was out of diapers? He'd thought it would be five or six months, maybe, but not too much longer than that.

How could he insist that Sophia change Hailey's diaper every hour after she'd pointed out that doing so would be harmful to the environment?

Damn, but he hated feeling inadequate and ignorant, and that's all he'd felt since his daughter had been tossed into his arms when she'd only been a few days old. How was he supposed to know how often a baby made poo?

"May I make a suggestion?" she asked.

He remained silent. He had a strong suspicion that nothing he said would keep this woman from offering her idea.

"How about if I promise to check the baby's diaper every hour? No, every thirty minutes." She tilted her cute oval face to one side. "The moment I detect any dampness, I'll whip that diaper off and clean her little bottom. Cross my heart, I will."

She made a small *x* on her chest, just above her left breast. And a nicely rounded breast it was, too. He jerked his gaze to the floor, blinked and silently ordered himself to focus.

As he sat there listening to her revising his guidelines, his attention wavered. This was exactly the type of woman he'd been trying to avoid. She was personable, charming…and manipulative. Not to mention beautiful and sexy. A woman who appealed to a man in every sense of the word.

Oh, she'd shown up at his door looking much different than she had in her office. Then, her thick chestnut hair had curled softly around her shoulders, and shiny lipstick had made her mouth glisten. She'd tied her hair back and washed her face, but her sparkling blue eyes didn't need any more highlighting other than the thick, fanning lashes and the dainty dark eyebrows arching above them.

She was an attractive woman, with or without cosmetics. And she had a body that wouldn't quit. Her knee-length skirt didn't hide her shapely calves and petite ankles. And there were plenty of curves beneath that jacket and blouse; a man didn't have to possess an overabundance of imagination to envision them.

The realization that he'd become keenly aware of her physical attributes scared the hell out of him. He was a business professional who worked with women every day. He was well-acquainted with proper conduct.

"I think we should talk about Hailey's feeding times," Sophia said easily.

Her tone plainly conveyed that she felt the schedule was up for discussion, and that irked Michael.

She lowered the typed pages and rested them on her shapely thighs. "Don't you think she ought to tell us when she's hungry, rather then us telling her when she's going to eat? It's much healthier for her to eat only when the need arises. Don't you think?"

Her tone was amiable and sincere enough, but that final little three-word query had been added on as if it were some sort of conciliation. If there was one thing he hated it was being placated. It smacked of collusion, and he'd been there, done that, and had no intention of repeating the experience, thank you very much.

She crossed her legs then, and the papers slid from her lap. She caught them along with the fabric of her skirt, and she ended up lifting the hem several inches, revealing cute dimpled knees. She quickly smoothed the fabric back into place. The entire incident was over in a fraction of a second, but Michael's mouth went dust dry.

This was the kind of situation that had gotten him into this mess. He'd gotten mixed up with a manipulative woman who used her wiles to get what she wanted. He had to stop this. Now.

"I can see that this isn't going to work out." He shoved himself out of the chair and stalked to the far side of the living room. "What the hell did I say to you this morning that made you think Hailey's schedule is negotiable? Wait. Don't bother answering that. I know I've been nothing but absolutely clear about what I want and expect from you and your business. I can't have this." He raked his fingers through his hair, and in a firmer voice, he said, "I won't have it. I'm sorry, but I have to terminate our contract. You can go. I'll make other arrangements for my daughter."

Surprise widened her eyes. He hated to admit it, but her alluring gaze stirred a lava-like heat down deep in his belly.

He didn't understand it. Normally, he was physically attracted to rawboned blondes. Curvy, dark-haired Sophia was neither. So what was this provocative rousing he was experiencing? Could he be confusing an acute irritation for something else? Something totally inappropriate?

The thought provoked a silent, unwitting nod.

Whether it was simple anger he was feeling, or something else, one thing was certain—he had to get rid of Sophia Stanton. And he had to get rid of her now.

"Hold on a second," she said. "Would you just lighten up? I didn't mean to make you angry. I wasn't *negotiating* the schedule. I was simply attempting to discuss it. You know, in an exchange of ideas."

"Semantics," he pointed out. "It's all the same thing."

"It most certainly is not."

But her gaze veered away from him even as she

tucked her arms tightly under her breasts. He couldn't help but notice how the huffy action lifted the ample mounds, accentuated the roundness of them. He swiped his fingers over his jaw as the errant thought that she might be trying to tempt him flitted through his brain.

He had to stop this kind of thinking. It was unreasonable and bordered on paranoia. Not every woman was as conniving as Ray Anne. Or as rash and immature as Lily. Still, he couldn't completely shut out his suspicions.

The ringing phone woke Hailey. He glanced down the hallway toward his daughter's nursery and then toward the telephone in the kitchen.

"Go ahead and answer that." Sophia got up from the couch and dropped the list of rules onto the coffee table. "I'll go see to the baby."

"It's someone from work. I'm sure of it. I should have been in there already."

"It's okay," she said. "Take the call." Then she started down the hallway toward the back of the condo.

He watched for a second, impressed that even though he'd just canceled his contract with the woman she hadn't hesitated to offer her help. He was also impressed with the way her bottom swayed when she walked.

Immediately, he shook the thought from his head and went to answer the phone. Sure enough, his secretary was calling to alert him that a couple of his less experienced employees had questions before they could get started working this morning.

"I've got a problem here, Jen," he said. "Tell all four of the new hires to go into the simulator and answer the investing questions. Be prepared to hear them grumble because they completed the program once already, but going over the course again will be good practice. No one achieved a perfect score when they tested last week. Tell them that anyone scoring one hundred percent has lunch on me."

"You know how competitive they are," Jen warned. "You'll be buying four meals. What's the problem there? Is Hailey ill?"

"She's fine. I've got nanny problems."

"You've sure had plenty of those," his secretary commented.

"Tell me about it."

"The placement service you're using has a great reputation. Everyone says so. I'm surprised you're having such trouble."

"Frankly, so am I. But things will turn around soon. I've broken my relationship with the service and plan to hire my own nanny. Things should look up from here on out."

Having actually formulated a plan and spoken the words aloud, Michael felt once again in control of the situation. He liked to be in charge of things, liked to command his own destiny. He promised Jen he'd arrive at the office by noon before hanging up.

"So I really am fired."

He turned at the sound of Sophia's voice. He hadn't suspected she'd been in the kitchen doorway eavesdropping on his phone conversation.

She shot him a sheepish smile. "I patted Hailey's bottom and she fell right off back to sleep. And her diaper was dry. I checked." Then she added, "I wasn't snooping on you. Honest, I wasn't. I just happened in at the tail end of your call."

Sophia took two steps into the kitchen, and he

watched her smooth her fingertips over the shiny granite countertop.

"I do wish you'd reconsider," she said. "I've never been fired before. And I know you won't believe it, but I've never had a single dissatisfied client."

"Until now." He moved to the sink, picked up the coffee cup he'd used earlier this morning and put it into the dishwasher. "I understand your position. But you have to understand mine. I expect certain things from the people I employ. And I wasn't getting those things from the nannies you sent."

He restrained himself from commenting that he seriously doubted he'd get them from her, either.

"I think it's best if I hire my own nanny," he said.

"And you think you're going to find one before noon today?"

Something twinkled in her big blue eyes, as if she had a big secret that no one else was privy to. What was it with this woman that she had to question his every move?

He certainly hadn't gotten to where he was by allowing naysayers to influence him. But something about this vivacious woman had him wanting to prove that he knew exactly what he was doing…even though he damn well didn't.

"That's exactly what I intend to do," he told her. "You're not the only nanny placement service in Wilmington."

"Actually, I am. That's why I started my business here. There are several in Philadelphia. But I seriously doubt they'll send their nannies this far south."

Refusing to allow this information to daunt him, he quickly regrouped. "I'll start with temp agencies, then. Surely, they can supply someone to watch Hailey."

There was warning written all over her face. "I doubt that temp agencies do background checks on their employees."

"I'll check the newspaper, then." She made him feel as if he were standing on shaky ground. "Someone has to be in need of a job."

"Yes, but who is that someone?" Sophia asked. "I doubt you want just anyone caring for Hailey. If you contact someone through an ad in the paper, I strongly suggest you do a thorough investigation. You'll need to give the person a letter stating you're offering them a job that requires a background search, and send them to the state police. Troop two in New Castle County is the only place you can get it done in northern Delaware. The police will fingerprint the person, take the necessary information and then you'll be sent a report."

Sophia was offering him some excellent information, suggesting things he hadn't even thought of. In fact, he wished he'd had a pen and paper on hand to jot down notes. Why was he feeling so damn irritated with her when all she was doing was continuing to be helpful?

"Of course," she added, "you'll have to wait ten to fourteen business days to receive the all-clear from the police."

There it was again. That glimmer in her gaze. She seemed to enjoy delivering news that put a damper on his plans. Obviously, she realized there was no way he could wait two weeks before hiring someone to care for Hailey.

He rejoiced when an idea popped into his head. "I can send her to a day care temporarily until I'm able to find someone and get the background check completed."

Sophia shook her head. "I doubt you'll find a day care that's willing to take a baby under six months old, and even if you do, infant spots are always on reserve. You'll have to wait six, eight—" she shrugged "—ten weeks, maybe."

He frowned. "You have an awful lot of doubts."

"I'm only trying to help," she told him.

"For some reason," he murmured, "I have grave doubts about that."

She chuckled, and the clear buoyancy he heard in it sent a strange tremor through his gut.

Confusion forced him to ask, "What's funny?"

Her expression straightened. "Your joke. You just complained that I had lots of doubts. Then you said you have doubts." She lifted her shoulders. "It was a cute joke."

"It wasn't a joke."

She blinked. "Oh."

She stood there, smiling. Then her smile slowly grew to a wide grin.

Michael had never thought of himself as dense. Quite the contrary. To achieve success in the cutthroat investment business, a person had to have intelligence, a quick wit and nerves of steel. However, he was left feeling quite lacking, indeed, when realization slowly dawned.

"Okay, I've figured it out." His jaw tensed as he released a frustrated sigh.

Now he knew why her tone had reflected such self-confidence, even when he'd been in the midst of firing her. Now he knew why humor had sparkled in her eyes, and why she stood there grinning.

"No other nanny placement services in the city." He began ticking off the list on his fingers. "No proper temp agency employees available. No newspaper ads to help. No background checks for two weeks. No day care that will agree to take my newborn daughter."

He'd wanted to get rid of her. Not because he didn't think she could care for Hailey. Oh, no. Not at all. His reasons for wanting her out of his home were far more personal in nature.

He leaned his hip against the cabinet. "You've known all along that I'm stuck with you? At least for the time being."

Mischief skittered across her gaze and tugged at the corners of her luscious mouth. "Well, I'll admit that I haven't known *all* along." She grinned openly. "But I feel I do have the right to feel pretty smug simply because I figured it out before you."

Chapter Three

Just as Sophia slipped on her jacket, Michael entered the living room.

"You're leaving?" He actually looked startled.

"Well, yes," she told him. "It's Saturday. I'm off today and tomorrow. I was going to come find you before I left. Tell you that Hailey was only up a couple of times through the night. She should awaken early this morning." She picked up her purse. "I'm off to check on my cat. Pick up my mail. Check with my assistant that everything's okay at the office. I have laundry to do, a few errands to run and—"

"Of course. Of course. Everyone deserves time off."

The trepidation edging his words was unmistakable.

"Michael, you're not afraid to be alone with Hailey, are you?" Instantly, she realized she'd made a poor choice of words. A dynamic man like Michael didn't appreciate the inference that he might be fearful—of anything. Some quick rephrasing was certainly in order. "What I meant to say was that you have no reason to be uncomfortable with your daughter." A tiny furrow bit into her forehead as she pointed out, "The other nannies you've employed had weekends off. I'm sure they did."

He nodded. "And every weekend has been two days of hell."

Sophia smiled. "Surely you're exaggerating."

But he didn't return her smile. "I honestly believe Hailey and I make each other nervous. She gets cranky. I get edgy."

"Oh, come on. Hailey's a good baby. She's been calm and easygoing for me since I moved in on Thursday. And she's been great for you in the evenings, too." Meaning only to inject a little humor, she added, "I could tell you some stories about children who were suspected of being true devil-spawn." She chuckled, and he did have the grace to smile, albeit fleetingly.

"Besides the fact that your daughter's so laid-back," she continued, "you've done great with her over the past couple of days. You've made great strides. You've learned to feed her properly. You've bathed her." She grinned. "And I haven't had a single diaper fall off her little butt since I showed you how to fit them more snugly."

Again he nodded. "I know. And you're right. I'll be fine. I'm sure."

He didn't sound sure.

Just then Hailey's cry came from down the hall.

"Sounds like Her Majesty is awake," Sophia quipped.

"I'd better get in there." He glanced behind him, distracted by the baby. "You have a great weekend."

"Thanks. I'll see you bright and early Monday morning."

Hailey's cries swiftly elevated to wails, and Michael's gaze collided with Sophia's. In an instant, he seemed to be standing on the threshold of panic.

Calmly, she remarked, "Sounds to me like a 'my-diaper's-wet-and-I-don't-like-it' cry and a 'feed-me-now' cry all rolled into one." She set her purse down. "You change her diaper and I'll get her bottle ready."

At first, she thought he might reject her offer of help. But obviously he was too smart for that.

"Okay," he agreed. "But as soon as she's settled, you can go. We'll be all right. I know you have things to do."

She answered him with an easy nod and they went off in different directions.

As the bottle was warming, Sophia thought back over the time she'd spent in Michael's home. She'd arrived feeling angry and resentful over his treatment of the women she'd placed in his home to care for Hailey. The nannies had described him as harsh and bossy and superior, and Sophia had bore the brunt of that behavior from him, too. But what those young women hadn't seemed to grasp was that there was a logical reason behind The Beast's growling exterior. Sophia suspected his controlling, inflexible conduct regarding his daughter was due more to his feelings of paternal inadequacy than it was his need to flaunt his authority as their employer. Of course, Sophia would never try to delude herself. He was a complicated man whose strong personality could never be completely comprehended— not in just two short days, at least. However, he had proven to her that he was willing to compromise, although she had pushed the issue a time or two. Although his list of rules remained in plain sight so they wouldn't be forgotten, Michael had made concessions on some of the sillier ones. In fact, just last evening the three of them had taken a stroll to the park.

Sophia thought it funny, the many times over the past few days he'd staunchly referred to the information he'd read in the outdated parenting manual he'd been using as a reference. Patiently, she had worked to show him that there was a huge difference in reading instructions printed in a book and in the real, hands-on experience of caring for a newborn. And he'd been an excellent pupil, as eager to learn as any other new father would be.

She placed a drop of the formula on the tender skin of her wrist and, finding the temperature to be perfect, she twisted the top back onto the bottle securely and headed toward the nursery. Michael was just then swaddling a cranky Hailey in her blanket as Sophia entered the room.

"Good morning, Hailey," Sophia called softly, peering around Michael's shoulder. The baby was too busy fussing to give her much notice. "Are you hungry, honey? I've got your breakfast right here."

Michael still looked a little freaked when he took the bottle she held out to him. Tucking his daughter in the crook of his arm, he said, "Let's go out into the living room. As soon as I can get her quiet, you can go."

"I'm in no hurry," she assured him. Any other response would have only added to his anxiety. Besides, she spoke the truth.

He went down the hall, murmuring softly to Hailey. Walking behind him, Sophia couldn't help but notice how he was dressed. He looked good in the business suits he wore during the work week. But today he was dressed very casually. The horizontal hunter-green piping that spanned the upper back of his cream-colored polo shirt emphasized his broad shoulders. The denim

fabric of his jeans hugged his muscular thighs. The man
had a great body.

Sophia forced her gaze northward when they entered
the living room, but even then her thoughts went
wayward. Hailey's howling wasn't enough of a distrac-
tion to keep her from noticing how appealing Michael's
tawny hair looked where it met the tanned flesh of his
neck. Unwittingly, she rubbed the tips of her fingers
against the pad of her thumb, wondering what the short
hair at the nape of his neck would feel like. Bristly? Or
silky soft?

Heat rushed to her face just as he sank down onto the
leather couch. He merely touched the nipple to the baby's
pink lips and Hailey began rooting frantically for suste-
nance. Sophia heard her take two loud, slurping gulps and
she reached down, slid her fingers over Michael's hand
and pulled the bottle from Hailey's mouth. Surprise had
him tipping up his chin to looking questioningly at her.

"Don't let her drink too fast," Sophia warned.
"She'll swallow air and end up spewing her breakfast
all over you."

Some strange voltaic current tingled her skin where
it contacted his. She pulled her hand away slowly so as
not to draw attention to her reaction, her fingers curling
into a fist all on their own.

Hailey cried out in her frenetic search for food.

"We need to calm her." Sophia smoothed the backs
of her fingers against Hailey's warm, fuzzy head. "Go
ahead and try the bottle again. But see if rocking her
very gently will help her relax a little."

This time Hailey settled in, seemingly contented by
the soothing, swaying motions. Sophia traced the round
outline of Michael's biceps muscle with her eyes.

"She is sweet, isn't she?"

The deep resonance of his voice caused Sophia to go still. Again, her face suffused with warmth. He thought she'd been staring at Hailey.

"Yes," she said, the words coming with difficulty. "Very." Sophia slipped around the coffee table and perched herself on the edge of the sofa next to him. She noticed he was staring at her, intently, and her first reaction was to look away. But she held his gaze.

"You know, when I first brought Hailey home from the hospital I was so ill-equipped and unprepared to be a parent that all I could see her as was a new responsibility." His brow furrowed slightly. "The idea of 'getting it right,' of doing everything correctly, overwhelmed me to the point that I was actually missing out on a lot—the joy she brings me, the contentment she's awakened inside me, the delight she stirs to life when I think that I made her. That she's a part of me."

He looked a little embarrassed to have confessed his feelings.

"Babies are amazing little miracles," Sophia said. Something inside her pinched almost painfully. She'd long ago decided against having any "little miracles" of her own.

"I have you to thank for the change in my attitude," he said.

"Me?" She tugged off her cardigan and set it on the cushion beside her. "But I haven't been here long enough to do that."

"Oh, but you have. You've taught me a lot. I don't mind admitting it. You helped me to relax." He chuckled. "Oh, I realize that I still have moments of sheer panic—this morning was a great example—but I am getting better. And it was only after I loosened up that I was able to begin to see and feel and understand what this little girl means to me."

She studied him, recognizing that he was exposing an important revelation.

"You know," he continued, "I now understand that, yes, Hailey does require a lot of care, but as I was putting her to bed last night I realized she gives something back, too."

Unable to come up with a fitting response, Sophia just smiled. Then she said, "Michael, as a new parent, you really do need to think about creating a support system for yourself. The stronger, the better. Usually, husbands and wives have each other, but…"

The subject of Hailey's absent mother hadn't come up between them, even though Sophia had been very curious. And, just as she'd suspected, mentioning it made her feel quite awkward. He was a private person. Drawing information from him wasn't easy. Besides that, his personal life was really none of her business.

"I don't have that," was all he said.

"How about asking your parents—"

"They can't help me. Not right now. They're on an extended trip they've looked forward to for a very long time. My father retired just a couple of months ago. They're touring the country in their RV, and planning to visit every state in the continental U.S. I refuse to be the reason they don't achieve their dream."

Sophia was a strong advocate of working with what was available, so she suggested, "Okay, so maybe you need to turn to friends. Friends who have children, of course. You need someone to talk to. Someone to share experiences with, someone who's going through the same thing you are."

"I understand what you're saying—" he kept his gaze fastened to his daughter's face "—but I don't have any."

Sophia grinned. "I find it a bit difficult to believe you have no friends."

When he looked at her, laughter glittered in his dark eyes. "I should have clarified. No friends with children."

"Ah, I see." She pondered. "Maybe I'll do a little research. I might be able to find a group for single parents at a local church or maybe through social services with the city. Would you be interested in something like that? Meeting other people in your same situation might offer you some—"

"I seriously doubt you'll find anyone else in my particular situation."

The cryptic remark made Sophia grow quiet. She hoped he'd elaborate. But he didn't. Finally, she could stand it no longer.

"It's clear," she said haltingly, reluctant to broach the subject, but feeling it necessary, "that you have full custody of Hailey. Is that because her mother died giving birth to her?"

He shook his head, his focus on Hailey. "She's alive and well, as far as I know."

"Then I'm baffled," Sophia continued. "There hasn't been a single call from her mother. Not a single visit. I just can't imagine any mother not wanting to see her child. It's not natural. I'm sorry for butting into your personal business, Michael, but it's just not... *normal.*"

His expression tightened until he looked almost grim. She feared he was going to take her head off for raising a subject that was evidently very sore.

"You've summed up Hailey's mother quite fittingly,

I'd say." He shifted the baby in his arms. "There isn't much about Ray Anne that would remotely resemble normal."

Wow. The interesting remark churned up several questions in Sophia's mind.

Was he speaking literally? Did this Ray Anne suffer with some kind of mental condition? Or was he being facetious? Was she perfectly sound of mind, yet some kind of oddball? If so, how had he become involved with such a woman?

He must have sensed the thoughts whizzing through her head because he frowned. "Look, Sophia, you can't be surprised to learn that not all women have deep maternal instincts. Well, Ray Anne is one of those women. She's not interested in being a mother. She's not interested in being involved in Hailey's upbringing. She's not interested in being a part of her life at all. And I thank the good Lord for that every single day." His brown gaze went stony. "That's all I'll say on the matter."

The firm tone of his voice left her with the distinct impression that—although he didn't intend to say more—there was plenty more to be said. A small part of her curiosity had been satisfied, she had to admit, but what he'd revealed only stirred more questions in her mind about Michael and this mysterious woman named Ray Anne.

He pulled the nipple from Hailey's milky lips, lifted her to his shoulder and began patting her gently on the back. Uncomfortable silence stretched out between them. Sophia was only supposed to have stayed this morning until Hailey had calmed down. Well, it looked as if she'd done just that. It also looked as if Michael was well in control of the situation.

"Okay, then—" she stood up "—I guess I should be on my way."

"I'm sorry I kept you so long."

He didn't look at her, and she regretted that the air between them had taken on an unwieldy feel.

"It's okay," she stressed. "I didn't mind at all." She moved around the coffee table and the uneasiness only seemed to swell. She made her way to the foyer and picked up her purse from the table by the front door. "I'll see you Monday morning."

He nodded once, and she left.

The ringing came from somewhere far off in the distance. So far off that Sophia was able to ignore it. She sank back into the comforting depths of sleep. The dream ensnaring her was vaporous and vague, but the hints of eroticism were unmistakable; a man's warm touch on her bare skin, his powerful, dark gaze filled with sensuous promise, his moist lips brushing secret places, rousing a profound and hungry need in her.

But the ring remained insistent, dragging her reluctantly into consciousness. Instinct had her reaching for the phone receiver before she was fully awake.

"Mmm," she murmured.

"Sophia, it's Michael."

She sighed. Michael. A smile curled her mouth as she remembered his warm, skillful hands on her bare skin.

Adrenaline shot through her body. She sat up in bed, alert and wide-eyed, her heart skittering behind her ribs.

"Michael."

"I'm sorry to call so early."

Her gaze swung to the clock. It was just after five in the morning.

"Is everything okay?" she asked. "Is Hailey hurt? Is she sick?"

"She's not hurt. And I don't think she's sick."

"You don't sound sure."

"That's because I'm not."

"Does she have a fever? Is she throwing up? Is she breathing okay?"

She shot the questions at him like bullets from a semiautomatic. He answered each one negatively.

"She's been fretful all weekend," he told her. "She hasn't slept well. She's not eating like she should. Like she did when...well, when you were here."

Some odd warmth bloomed in her chest like a crimson rose, and Sophia tossed back the blanket and sheet.

"I'll be right there," she told him.

"You don't mind?"

"Of course not," she said, hearing the gratitude in his tone. "It's Monday morning. I'd be coming to your house in a few hours anyway. Let me jump in the shower. I'll be there within the hour."

True to her word, Sophia arrived at Michael's condo just before six. She rapped on the front door and then let herself in with the key.

Surprised at the quiet, she passed through the foyer and went into the living room. Her eyebrows arched high and she smiled at the state of things. A bath towel was tossed over one black leather chair. A coffee cup and a water glass sat on one end table. Two newspapers had been tossed on the couch, and both were so neatly folded that she could tell that neither had been read. The television remote was peeking out from behind a chair leg. One of Michael's dress shirts was on the floor under the coffee table, along with a pair of dark socks. A bowl with bits of dried food sat on a small table next to the kitchen door. The room was a mess, and a quick glance told her the kitchen was in much the same disarray.

Michael padded down the hall toward her, barefoot, his hair disheveled. His white T-shirt and burgundy-striped cotton pajama pants were rumpled. He was unshaven, and he looked exhausted.

"You weren't lying," she teased, "when you told me you're not very good at this parenting thing."

"Good morning to you, too," he grumbled. But her comment caused him to take a moment to look around. He shook his head and chuckled. "I wasn't lying, was I?"

Sophia set her purse down. "So where's the princess?"

"You won't believe what happened."

"Let's have some coffee," she suggested, "while you tell me." Her eyes lit mischievously. "You look like you could use some."

Automatically, he combed his fingers through his tawny hair and then ran his hand over his stubbly jaw.

In the kitchen, she reached over the dirty dishes for a fresh coffee filter while Michael rustled up two clean mugs.

"I can't believe how quickly my house became a wreck," he said. "It's next to impossible to get anything done."

Sophia empathized. "I'll see if I can clean up a bit. Here and there. While she's napping today."

"Oh, no. I can't let you do that," he told her, his tone emphatic. "It's my mess. I made it, I'll clean it up."

She poured water into the machine while he measured ground coffee into the lined basket. Sophia snapped the switch and the coffeemaker began heating up. "We make a good team."

"We do, don't we?" He moved to the table and pulled out a chair, motioning for her to join him.

"So what was this unbelievable happening?" She sat down and rested her elbows on the table.

"First of all," he said, "I want to apologize for waking you. But I was at my wit's end. Hailey had been up most of the night. Not crying, really, just…fitful. Unable to sleep."

Reaching across the table, Sophia touched him. "There's no need to apologize. I'm actually glad you felt you could call on me for help."

Appreciation eased his gaze as he studied her silently. Then she became acutely aware of the warmth of him, and realized her fingers were still curled around his corded forearm. She drew back.

"I thought at first that she might be catching a cold," he explained. "She just couldn't seem to get comfortable. She refused to fall asleep in her crib. So I walked the floor with her. She'd drop off, but as soon as I put her down, she'd wake up and we'd start all over."

"It's very hard to say sometimes why babies—"

"But I think I figured it out," he said, excitement brightening his expression as he cut her off. "No, I'm sure I did."

As the rich scent of coffee filled the air, Sophia waited for him to give her more details of his experience with his daughter.

He got up and went to the counter. "After I called you—" he poured coffee into one mug and then the other "—I laid Hailey down on the couch just to give myself a little breather. I really needed a break. And suddenly, she went really quiet."

Sophia took the coffee he offered, but couldn't keep the curiosity she felt from creasing her forehead.

"It was your sweater," he told her. "You left it here on Saturday. It was draped on the cushion beneath Hailey. She calmed right down. You calmed her down. Or rather, the scent of you did. I'm sure of it. I hope you don't mind, but I tucked your sweater around her once she fell off to sleep. It's in her room. In her crib with her."

Sophia tipped a spoon of sugar into her coffee. "I guess the smell of me could have quieted her." Although she had her doubts, she didn't voice them because she didn't want to put a damper on his excitement. "I guess it's possible she could have gotten used to having me around." After only two days? She didn't think so.

But he beamed despite his obvious fatigue. "I can't believe I figured it out."

The spoon clinked against the side of the ceramic mug as Sophia slowly stirred her coffee. "That's what parenting is." She smiled. "An unrelenting series of puzzles that need figuring out."

Michael shook his head. "And to think…this puzzle only took me two days to solve."

She chuckled. "If it makes you feel any better, I would have had to do the same thing you did. Trust dumb luck to finally show up."

"Ah," he said, lifting his index finger, "but you were what she wanted. So this wouldn't have happened to you."

"Maybe." She sipped the coffee, closing her eyes for an instant to savor the taste. "But you can bet that while I'm with her today, another dilemma will arise. And I'll have to rely on dumb luck to figure it out."

They shared a chuckle, and Sophia became cognizant of an underpinning stir, a slight, heated tremor that pulsed in the air. Something in her mind warned her not to ponder it too closely, warned her to completely ignore it. But there was one thing she simply couldn't ignore, and that was the realization that, despite her interrupted night's sleep and the ungodly hour, she felt quite satisfied. Happy, even.

She laced her fingers around the warm mug, thinking some more teasing was in order. "Is there someplace where I can make a note of your transgression?"

Her question so bewildered him that she laughed. "You've broken one of your own rules. You're not wearing a robe."

He looked down at himself and groaned. "I'm sorry, Sophia. I was so tired, I didn't even notice."

He made to get up but she stopped him with a shake of her head. "It's all right. Really. I'm not offended in the least." She grinned. "I don't find your pajamas and T-shirt the least bit indecent."

They drank their coffee, and Michael looked at her over the rim of his mug. The atmosphere in the kitchen seemed to compress.

"Now that you know how miserable I've been this weekend," he said, his comment taking on a captivating lilt, "may I ask how yours went?"

"You may," she told him, matching his campy cadence. "I had a great weekend. Not all that restful, but I accomplished a lot. My bills are paid, my apartment is clean, my laundry's done and Flicker and I had a lovely visit."

"Flicker?"

"My cat," Sophia said. "He's staying with my assistant while I'm here."

Michael nodded. "Yes, you did mention your cat on Saturday."

"I did. Flicker's an overweight tabby with a sweet-as-sugar attitude. Oh, and she's very wise."

Michael grinned, and Sophia realized he seemed more at ease now than she'd ever seen him. Surely that was because he'd tackled a sticky problem with Hailey and had conquered it—all on his own. She had to admit, there was something very appealing about him now that he was smiling, relaxed and confident. He seemed much more approachable.

"I didn't know cats could be wise. Superior. And disdainful. But wise?" His brown eyes glittered with humor.

"Oh, yes." Her head bobbed. "Some cats can be quite stupid, but Flicker is highly intelligent. We talk, you know."

He looked as if he enjoyed her silliness.

"We talked about you this weekend," she continued.

"This is getting better." He shifted on the chair and leaned toward her just enough to show his interest. "And what did your fat, smart tabby have to say about me?"

"Well, Flicker thinks my suggestion for a support system is a good one," Sophia said. "And since Hailey's mom isn't available to help—" she rushed past that sore subject "—I think you should ask your mom to come help you for a while."

"But you're here to help," he said. Then he frowned. "Are you trying to tell me something? Are you handing in your resignation as Hailey's nanny?"

"Of course not. I wouldn't do that. It's just that I think that, having raised at least one child of her own, your mother could help you a lot. I'm sure she'd have some wonderful motherly advice to offer, if you'd give her a chance."

He looked away. "But I've already told you that my parents—"

"I know what you said. Your parents are traveling."

Sophia loosened her grip on her coffee mug. "But I think this is more important. Their granddaughter will only be brand-new for a little while. You'll only need your mom and dad for a little while, too. They can travel later, Michael." She smiled. "The country will still be there, you know."

Something dark clouded his countenance…his whole demeanor. Guilt?

Finally, he swung his frowning gaze to hers and quietly confessed, "I haven't told them."

Several seconds ticked by as she sat there. "I don't understand. You haven't told them what?" Realization slowly sank in and with it came astonishment. "You haven't told your parents about Hailey? They don't know you have a daughter?" Incredulity made each question roll off her tongue at a higher octave. She shook her head. "B-but…*why not?*"

Michael's frown turned to a scowl.

"You're overstepping your bounds, Sophia," he said. "My personal life isn't your concern." He got up and set his mug next to the sink that was cluttered with dirty dishes. "I don't have any more time to talk. I have to shower and dress, and then I have to clean this place up. If I don't get started, I'll be late for work."

He walked out of the kitchen, leaving Sophia staring.

Chapter Four

By Wednesday evening, Sophia couldn't take the silence any longer. Monday and Tuesday after Michael had returned home from work, he'd spent a few moments cuddling his daughter, and then he'd busied himself at his desk in the room at the end of the hallway, leaving Sophia to care for Hailey. He hadn't even joined them for dinner. He'd followed the same routine this evening and was now hidden behind the closed door of his office. The tension in the condo was thick enough to choke her.

She'd butted into his personal life, probing into the subjects of his wife and his parents. He was making it perfectly clear that he wasn't happy about what he saw as her intrusion. She intended to apologize as soon as he presented himself long enough for her to do so.

However, right now what she needed was a release from the strain. So she bundled Hailey up in a fleece jumper that would protect her from the cool October breeze and tucked her into her stroller. She slipped into her jacket and then rapped on Michael's office door.

"No need to open," she called out. "I just wanted to let you know that I'm taking Hailey for a walk."

Sophia had pushed the stroller halfway down the hall when he pulled open the office door.

"Would you mind some company?"

She stopped, and turned to face him, unable to keep the surprise she felt from reflecting on her face. A challenging quality tinged his question; it was almost as if he were expecting her to deny him the opportunity to accompany her and Hailey. Well, that would never happen. He was the parent. He had every right to be with the baby.

"Would you like to take her?" Sophia asked. "I can stay behind."

"Actually, I'd like for us to go together. I think we should talk."

Brick-heavy dread gathered in the pit of her stomach, but at the same time she was relieved to get things out in the open. "Michael, I understand that I invaded your privacy. And I apologize. It won't happen again."

He frowned. "I was upset. I can't deny that. But you only spoke with my best interest in mind, Sophia. I'm smart enough to realize that much."

He paused, swallowed and then ran a hand across his jaw, his gaze never wavering from hers. She sensed that he was focused on some sort of mental deliberation.

"I'd like to…explain some things," he finally said.

There was something both hesitant and vulnerable in his comment.

"Just let me grab a jacket." He ducked into his bedroom.

Sophia wasn't sure how she should feel about this

surprising turn of events; however, because he remained silent as they made their way out the door and down the long, carpeted corridor, and he didn't speak a single word during the elevator ride to the lobby, a strange unease began to fill her. Suddenly she wasn't sure that she wanted him to explain anything, which was an odd feeling for her to have since she'd been curious about him and Hailey and their family situation ever since she'd come to work for him.

She didn't dare look at him as they walked down the sidewalk, side by side.

Autumnal ocher stained the edges of the leaves. It was that time in the early evening when the city streets were nearly empty and quiet. Only an occasional car passed by them as they strolled toward no place in particular.

Michael inhaled deeply, and then he gave the kind of cough that wasn't really a cough, but an obvious sign that he was about to speak.

"Money and success are new to me. What I mean is, I come from a blue-collar background."

His assertion baffled Sophia. Of all the things she'd been expecting to hear, this information hadn't even made the list.

"My father retired," he continued, "from the Chrysler assembly plant in Newark. That's where I grew up. I attended school there. Dad was a foreman on the line for over thirty years, and he worked hard—I'm talking about strenuous, physical labor—in order to earn a living for his family. My mother was mainly a stay-at-home mom. She did take part-time jobs occasionally over the years. We were most definitely middle class, and I remember times when my parents had a difficult time making ends meet."

She sensed rather than saw his rueful smile.

"Those were the times," he said softly, "that Mom would take a temporary job as a clerk in the local five-and-dime," he said. "Or she'd type letters for one of the lawyers in town. What I'm trying to say is that I didn't come from money or privilege."

Why his childhood economics were so important, Sophia had no idea. But Michael wasn't the kind of person to reveal personal information without good, sound reason. She had sense enough to realize the man was on his way to making a point.

"I realized in high school," he continued, "that I had a knack with numbers. And I soon discovered that I excelled in matters of money and economics. Finance. Investing. That kind of thing. I earned a degree from the University of Delaware, and went right to work."

In one unceremonious motion, he curled his fingers round the handle of the stroller very near hers. Sophia's gaze riveted to the back of his hand. She noticed the small, corded muscles playing just beneath his skin. She wondered how warm he'd feel if she were to slide her palm over his fingers. Sophia did her best to push the errant thought from her mind. She shifted her gaze, focusing on the concrete walkway passing beneath the rubber wheels of Hailey's stroller.

"What I learned really quickly—" his hand left the stroller handle and swung naturally at his side "—is that there are many people who want to invest their money, but very few of them have the knowledge and confidence to put their desire into action. People were willing to pay me huge sums of money to increase their portfolio. Within six months, I was in charge of a whole team of young investors."

Money matters often overwhelmed Sophia. She remembered when she'd started The Nanny Place, she'd been scared to death about taking out the loan that enabled her to open her office. The start-up costs had seemed astronomical. So had the risk. She'd feared that, like so many other small companies, she would have to fold up shop before she'd completed her first year in business. But after twelve grueling months, she'd turned a small profit, and before too long, she'd succeeded in gaining enough return business that she'd been able to hire Karen, her assistant, on a part time basis. Slowy, but surely, The Nanny Place had grown from a struggling business to a fairly prosperous one.

Michael must be talented, indeed, to have attained so much success so quickly.

Turning her head, she glanced at his profile. She'd already realized he was a handsome man. But she was seeing him a little differently this evening. She was learning more about him. And she was finding out something about herself, too. She was just discovering that she found braininess in a man damn sexy.

His voice dropped to nearly a whisper as he added, "The windfall I found came very unexpectedly."

Not wanting him to see her bewildered frown, she shifted her head forward. She'd never seen this side of Michael. Before this moment, her only perception had been that he was a dominant and compelling individual who knew exactly what he wanted and wouldn't rest until he got it. But now he seemed hesitant, almost unsure of himself.

"Success isn't a bad thing," she felt impelled to murmur. She'd had to work very long and hard to find hers.

"It can be. If you let it go to your head let it affect your behavior."

Sophia tucked her bottom lip between her teeth in order to stem her urge to ask him what he meant. She didn't speak, sensing his intention to explain.

They walked nearly a half block in silence, and with every step, she wanted to pry him open like a tin can. *Patience*, she silently scolded. *Have a little patience*.

Finally, he offered, "I take my job seriously. I work hard. I always have. You can't mess around when you're handling money that belongs to others. Someone's entire life savings can be lost in the blink of an eye, with one careless mistake on my part."

Birds twittered in the branches of the oaks that had been planted along the grassy area separating the street and sidewalk.

"But I do have to admit," he said, "that in order to blow off steam…in order to reduce the stress of my job, I picked up the habit of playing hard, too."

By this time they had reached a small common area that had several benches and a gurgling fountain. She pointed to a bench, offering a silent invitation to sit, which he answered with a nod.

They sat, turning the stroller so that they were within Hailey's view. The baby seemed content to listen to the bubbling water and watch the world around her.

Michael took a deep breath. "My newfound affluence offered me a new and awfully exciting lifestyle. New friends seemed to crop up everywhere I went. People from a whole different social status wanted to hang out with me. Guys inviting me to Philly for an Eagles game, or to get together at a sports bar to watch the Knicks play, or meet for a game of poker. And the women…" He let the rest of the sentence trail as he shook his head.

"It might be terrible," he said, "but I must confess that I didn't mind being actively pursued. But, quite frankly, all of it went to my head, Sophia. Over the last few years I've dated more women than I can count. Than I can even remember."

He hooked his ankle over his knee. "And being a normal, red-blooded male, I was proud to have beautiful women on my arm when I was attending different social events, or even if I was simply going out for dinner and a movie."

Sophia glanced at Hailey and saw that the baby's eyes had fluttered closed, her tawny lashes fanning out on her milky cheeks.

"But I learned recently," he said, "that a man with his head in the clouds can't see what's going on around him."

He went quiet, and Sophia's curiosity got the better of her. "I can't decide—" one corner of her mouth curled upward when he looked her way "—if that statement is profoundly wise or terribly cryptic."

"I went stone stupid for quite a while." His tone was rueful when he said, "I was so caught up in the…well, in the unrestrained opportunities where women were concerned, that I allowed myself to fall into a very vulnerable position."

Leaning forward, Sophia straightened the blanket nestled around Hailey even though the pink cotton cover was already smooth. He'd exposed a tiny sliver of this vulnerability back at his home when he'd expressed his need to talk. Although she felt a little uncomfortable with all he was revealing about himself, it wasn't enough to override her interest in what he was saying.

"I'd thought I was being extremely careful," he told her, "when it came to—"

He stopped short, as if his thought had been snipped clean in two with sharp scissors. She stifled the urge to smile when she saw his face aflame with embarrassment. Now was no time to laugh at the man.

She quietly offered, "Sexual encounters?"

He nodded without looking at her. "Exactly," he murmured. Then he stressed, "I really was very careful."

Finally, Sophia was able to put a couple pieces of the puzzle together. She reached out and touched the stroller where his daughter slept. "But not careful enough?"

Again, he nodded. "When Ray Anne told me she was pregnant, I was dumbfounded. I didn't know what to say to her."

"Accidents happen, Michael. They happen more frequently than anyone realizes."

His tone was finely honed as he said, "Hailey was no accident."

Sophia leaned against the wooden slats of the bench's back, surprise lifting her eyebrows. "So this woman—Ray Anne—wanted to get married so badly that she purposefully became pregnant with your child?" Before he could answer, she sighed. "That happens all too often, too, I guess. Desperate women stoop to desperate measures."

He muttered, "Ray Anne was desperate, all right. But marriage wasn't part of her agenda. Raising a child wasn't, either."

Like an unexpected bombshell, this disclosure bewildered Sophia to the point of utter silence. She simply sat there next to him, frowning. If marriage hadn't been the woman's motive, and raising Hailey hadn't been, either, then what *had* been?

As if he'd actually heard the silent question echoing in her brain, Michael said, "Money. She requested a large monetary settlement in exchange for full custody of Hailey."

Unable to comprehend exactly what he was saying, Sophia whispered, "But that means she…" She wasn't able to bring herself to utter the rest of the thought.

"Sold her baby," Michael supplied, his tone flat. "She sold *our* baby, and all her rights to Hailey. To me."

Frenetic thoughts sent Sophia into a tailspin. She wasn't normally one to judge other people, but this Ray Anne didn't sound like a very nice person. She sounded like a complete nutcase, in fact.

"Can you now understand," he said, "why I haven't told my parents?"

Still trying to digest all the information, Sophia didn't speak. And apparently, he took her silence as a condemning estimation on her part.

"Sophia, my mom and dad are decent, hardworking people." He put both feet flat on the asphalt that covered the small commons. "They did their best to instill good values in me. They took me to church. They taught me—mainly through their own day-to-day conduct—that a person's behavior matters. That following right principles matters."

Agitation had him scrubbing at the back of his neck. "You think I want my parents to know I lost sight of everything they tried to teach me? Everything they believe in so deeply?"

She was quiet for a moment, and then, rather than answering his question, she asked a couple of her own. "You haven't told your parents about Hailey because you think they're going to be disappointed in you? You think they're somehow going to be disillusioned by the circumstances surrounding her birth?"

Firmly and emphatically, he answered, "Yes. And yes. However, I don't *think* they'll be disappointed and disillusioned, I *know* they will be."

An orange-tinted leaf fluttered on the air, settling on the seat between them. Absently, Sophia picked it up by the stem and twirled it.

"From everything you've said," she told him, "your parents are respectable and reasonable people. I don't know them, so I can't say how they'll react when you explain your situation. I can't say that they won't be—" she searched for a softer description than he'd used "—a little disenchanted to learn that you got caught up in your success. But don't you think the joy of learning that they're grandparents will far outweigh any upset they might experience?" Without waiting for him to respond, she supplied, "I certainly do."

She was glad she offered an answer because, seemingly, he intended not to; however, he did look pensive, as if he were truly considering what she'd said.

"Obviously," she continued, "you've met all the challenges that would ensure your daughter's future with you. I have no idea what Ray Anne's plans were had you decided not to give her the money she asked for, but you've proved your dedication to Hailey. And you continue to show your devotion and love for her every single day. I've seen it for myself. I'm sure your parents, given the chance, will see that, too."

Sophia let the leaf fall to the ground. "Hailey changed your life. From what you've explained, she changed it for the better. She—and the events surrounding her birth—forced you to really see yourself and your behavior. And you've acted on that."

His thoughts were churning—she could tell by the tiny crease between his eyebrows.

"Personally," she said, "I believe that your past behavior doesn't matter nearly as much as your present behavior, or as much as your future behavior. There's absolutely nothing you can do about the past, Michael. That's history, and it can't be changed. No matter how much we'd like it to be. Don't let it define you. It's the present and the future that matter. And it's the present and the future that your parents will react to—that's what will make them proud."

After a moment, he softly asked, "You really think they'll be happy to learn about Hailey?"

"Michael, they're grandparents. They'll be over-the-moon happy. They'll be dancing-a-jig happy. They'll be—"

"Okay, okay." He chuckled. "I get it."

She honed in on him with a serious gaze. "You do?"

"I really do." He stood. "Now, let's go home. I have a call to make."

Warm elation swam in Sophia's chest.

He'd been holed up behind the closed door of his office for nearly an hour. Having passed by a couple of times on her way to and from the nursery, Sophia could hear the deep resonance of his voice, although she couldn't make out what he was actually saying. Early on, she'd heard him laugh. Then his tone had lowered and grown serious. But he sounded calm. So she was hoping that was a sign that his conversation with his parents was going well.

She'd busied herself with the baby; preparing Hailey's final bottle for the day and feeding her, giving the baby a warm bath, spending some time just talking to her.

Sophia was amazed by how quickly she'd bonded with Hailey. The baby stirred deep and complex feelings in her. She'd been around children in the past. When she'd started The Nanny Place, her intention had been to provide a hands-off placement service only. However, her business had evolved, until she'd become a confidant to many of her nannies, a friend to whom they could turn, someone they could trust. Then circumstances arose that required her to act as liaison, an arbitrator between the nannies and the parents for whom they worked. She didn't mind taking on this job especially when the final result was a better understanding among everyone involved. And finally, when her business was really booming, she'd been forced to act as a fill-in for sick nannies when replacements couldn't be found.

So she did have experience with children. Even very young ones. But the heated emotions Hailey roused in her were overwhelming. Satisfying. Potent. And seemingly cavernous. She awoke each morning eager to see if Hailey was awake. Fervent joy filled her each time she picked up the baby, smelled her delicate scent. And after she'd bathed Hailey and dressed her for the night, Sophia found she didn't want the day to end.

Caring for Michael's daughter fulfilled her in ways she had never before experienced. She didn't understand it, she didn't try to, she only intended to enjoy her time here to the fullest.

Sophia was amazed by how quickly Hailey had bonded with her. Most people might tend to believe that infants Hailey's age were unaware of what was going on around them or of who was feeding them, changing their diapers and smiling down into their cribs when they awoke from a nap. But Sophia was certain that Hailey connected with her. The infant would gaze at her as if she were truly studying her, memorizing her features or dissecting her thoughts.

The idea wasn't all that silly. The fact that Michael claimed to have calmed Hailey over the weekend by wrapping her in Sophia's sweater was very telling. At first, she had doubted it. However, she was quickly coming to the conclusion that Hailey just might know her scent, that she could very well have been comforted by it, and for some reason, that information only added fuel to the delicious warmth that permeated Sophia's being when she cuddled the baby in her arms.

Looking down at Hailey's sleeping form, Sophia realized she'd been rocking the baby longer than she'd realized. She smiled, remembering how uptight Michael had been at the suggestion of these quiet "snuggle" times. He'd even had a rule limiting the amount of time a nanny should hold his daughter. He'd feared too much contact would spoil Hailey, but Sophia had countered by gently explaining that babies couldn't get enough hugs and cuddling, and that the love Hailey was shown developed her sense of self-worth even at this young age. A feeling of trustfulness was being developed in Hailey, as well as her sense of well-being and security. Sophia also pointed out that the person doing the rocking and snuggling never went away from the experience empty-handed. She sure didn't. But she was too self-conscious to reveal to him the maternal feelings she experienced while she was caring for his daughter. That wouldn't have been professional. However, she had persuaded him that he would benefit from spending lots of special bonding time with Hailey.

He'd looked so awkward the first few times he cradled the baby, cooing and talking to her, that Sophia had slipped out of the nursery to give him some privacy. However, she could tell afterward that he'd enjoyed himself; his smile came more easily. As the days passed, he spent more and more time with Hailey, and now he broke out into baby talk right in front of Sophia. This pleased her because she knew this new closeness would only enrich the father-daughter relationship Michael and Hailey would spend their life sharing.

Sophia gently placed the snoozing baby on the crib mattress, pulled a blanket up to cover her and then stole from the room, quietly closing the door of the nursery behind her.

Michael exited his office just as she released the doorknob. Instantly, his shoulders fell. "I missed saying good-night?"

Sophia nodded ruefully. "I tried to keep her awake, but she started yawning." Sophia smiled at the memory. "She couldn't keep her little eyes open a moment longer."

He took a step toward her and she asked, "So…how did it go?"

It was strange that she would feel so antsy about something that was really none of her business. Michael got close enough to her that she could smell the woodsy scent of his cologne.

"What was it you said?" His chocolaty eyes lit. "That they'd be—"

He moved so quickly, she only had time to gasp. He wrapped his arms around her waist, picked her up and twirled her around in a circle.

"Dancing-a-jig happy?"

He set her down, and she was so wobbly from shock that she instinctively reached up and placed her hands on his shoulders to steady herself.

"That's what they were, Sophia. Mom was squealing like a young girl, and Dad kept shouting, 'Congratulations!'"

"Shhhh," she scolded softly. "You'll wake the baby."

He looked contrite and murmured an apology. He remained close, though, whispering, "I can't believe how light I feel, Sophia. It's amazing." He smiled. "Keeping this from my parents has been weighing on me like a ton of wet cement."

That smile. Those eyes. Those perfect, dusky lips. She'd done her best to ignore them, to ignore *him*, since she'd taken this dang job. No, she had to be honest; not him. Ignoring him would have been impossible since she was working for the man.

What she'd been striving to disregard was the fascination she found in him, and the allure that so often sizzled in the air when he was near. So far, he hadn't seemed the least bit aware of what he did to her or how she felt, and if Sophia had anything at all to say about it, he never would.

How embarrassing! Not to mention totally unprofessional. She'd be mortified if he ever learned she was attracted to him. He paid her to take care of his daughter.

Just act naturally, a wise voice from somewhere in her head chimed.

"I knew they'd be pleased," she said. She hoped the breathlessness she heard in her words was a figment of her freaked-out imagination.

"They wanted to know everything."

The exhilaration sparking his gaze intrigued her. She knew she should somehow try to liberate herself from his embrace, but his hands were firmly on her hips. If she made a big deal of being close to him, she'd only succeed in allowing him to see…well, that this was a big deal to her.

She tried to relax. Tried to continue acting as if being this close to a man she found attractive was quite routine.

Silently, she groaned. Who was she kidding? She couldn't keep up this appearance for very long. She could feel the perspiration dampening her armpits with each passing second.

Why did he have to smell so good? Why did he have to look so good? Oh, but she was doomed to failure here. He was going to find her out. She just knew it.

Act natural! the voice in her head repeated.

"S-so," she said, "did you tell them? Everything, I mean?"

He nodded. "I told them everything. It wasn't easy, but I did it. And I'm glad I did it."

His dark eyes flashed with an intense and sudden awe. "And you were right, Sophia." He kept his tone hushed. "They were so swept away with the news of Hailey that they didn't dwell on any of the bad things I'd had to confess. They were…overjoyed."

She felt the heat of him through his cotton shirt. His shoulders were solid, and the urge flashed through her to run her palms over his biceps. Blinking, she forced herself to focus on his face.

"I'm so glad, Michael," she told him. "I couldn't imagine them being anything else."

"Yeah." The emotion in his gaze condensed. "I know you couldn't."

He studied her face, her eyes, her hair, her mouth.

The condo was eerily quiet. The air around them grew heavy, and Sophia felt as if she couldn't breathe.

"If you hadn't spoken up," he whispered, "I don't know how long I'd have waited to tell them."

The intensity in his gaze was disconcerting.

Desperate to lighten the mood, she quipped, "Oh, you couldn't have put it off forever. Can you imagine that conversation? Mom, you have a four year old granddaughter. Or, Dad, meet Hailey, she's twelve."

She chuckled, but the sound died quickly, snuffed out by the potent magnetism exuding from Michael.

"I'm trying to be serious here, Sophia." Ever so slowly, he inched closer to her.

Her heart pounded fiercely, and even though she tried to remain calm, her breathing became shallower.

"I can see that," she sighed, swiftly getting caught up in the vortex that seemed to spin crazily around them.

"I want you to know—"

He leaned in even closer. She could see specks of warm amber in his deep brown eyes.

"—how grateful I am."

She was going to utter his name sharply. She was going to plant her hand on his chest. She was going to lean away from him.

But she did none of those things.

The same silent voice that had just told her to act as if nothing were amiss now alerted her that something extraordinary was about to happen. However, there was no hint of warning this time. Only an odd enthrallment, luring her to surrender.

Desire, thick and heady, eddied around her ankles, swirled around her hips, her shoulders, her arms. Like a soundless tempest, it whipped about her face and neck, tearing at her, teasing her, taunting her.

He moistened his lips, parted them slightly, and she knew without a doubt he intended to kiss her. Yielding to the wicked, bewitching wind that sent her emotions roiling, she leaned forward and became one with the marvelous, seductive storm.

Chapter Five

Firm. Smooth. Hot. Moist. The impressions blazed through Sophia's brain like jolts of pure electricity. Michael's kiss was all of these things, and more.

He slid one hand up to cup her jaw, the heat of him deliciously searing. She wished she could feel his sultry swelter on every inch of her flesh.

His tongue skittered across her lips, and she felt it was the most natural thing in the world to part them for him. He delved inside in untamed exploration. Her body seemed to take on a life of its own; her knees went weak, her arms felt heavy, her heart palpitated, blood rushed through her veins at a dizzying rate.

He nibbled and tasted until she felt so breathless she feared she might black out, but she willed herself to focus. Between the myriad frantic thoughts crashing through her mind, she was cognizant enough to realize that missing a single nuance—a single touch of his fingers, of his lips, of his tongue—was not an option.

One of his hands had remained resting on her hip, but ever so slowly, he slid it up the side of her body. He stopped high on her torso, his fingers spanning toward her back, his thumb settled securely beneath her breast.

She felt achy with the need to be touched, shocked by her body's powerful reaction to him, but not so shocked that she was willing to say or do anything that might break the spell that held them in such a fierce and beguiling grip.

He whispered her name, soft, sultry, his silky breath brushing her cheek, and the tiny hairs at the nape of her neck raised.

The heat of him seemed to envelop her like a cloak. She closed her eyes, tipped her face upward. He stroked her forehead, and then her temple with what she believed was the tip of his nose. She heard him inhale, and then he expelled a muted moan of pleasure. It was the most erotic sound she'd ever heard.

Something strange happened to her sense of time. Seconds seemed to slog by, and that was perfectly all right with her. She was happy right where she was, doing exactly what she was doing.

"Hey," he whispered.

Feeling as though she were swimming her way out of a thick fog, Sophia had to force her eyes open. Her whole body felt heavy and fatigued, but at the same time, an energizing pulse thudded through her.

He looked as dazed as she felt.

"What are we doing?" He traced the outline of her ear with his finger, then ran it down the line of her jaw.

She wanted to close her eyes, to surrender to the

desire calling to her; however, she strained to remain focused. "I don't know." She paused long enough to swallow. "I honestly don't."

Without thought, she took a deep breath and then let her tongue skip across her bottom lip, and immediately she felt a longing to once again taste his kiss. But by this time, reason was beginning to clear the haze in her head, and the thudding in her bloodstream grew weaker.

Her voice was stronger when she asked, "What *are* we doing?"

The beginnings of a languid smile formed on his mouth. Then he must have noticed the fluster and panic that was swiftly taking her hostage.

He pulled his hands from her, and Sophia was keenly aware of how chilled her body felt on the spots where he'd been caressing her. He stepped back and her thighs felt suddenly cool. She hadn't been aware of just how tightly he'd been pressed up against her.

He blinked, his gaze clearer. Evidently, his good sense was returning, as well.

"Damn, Sophia…*damn*." His rusty whisper seemed saturated with confusion. He frowned. "I had no idea I was going to do that. It's just that I—"

"It's all right," she blurted. For some reason, she felt a desperate need to keep him from apologizing. She didn't understand why, but hearing him actually say he was sorry that he'd kissed her would have mortified her to the marrow of her bones.

"No, it isn't all right." He shook his head. "I was overwhelmed. I was feeling so good. You know, about having told my parents about Hailey."

He seemed to be working it out just as the words tripped off his tongue.

"They were so pleased," he continued. "And it was all your doing. You talked me into telling them. And I was grateful."

I was overwhelmed. I was grateful.

Those two statements were almost as bad as an apology. "Like I said," she told him, straightening her blouse, "it's all right. You got caught up in the moment. No harm done." She reached up and smoothed still-shaky fingers over her hair. "I'm glad everything worked out okay with your parents. I really am. Now, if you'll excuse me, I was about to go have a shower and settle in for the night."

"Of course." He backed away another step.

She bid him good-night and then headed for her room. She tried not to rush. She didn't want to look as though she were running from him.

Once she was securely behind the closed door of her bedroom, she eased down onto the edge of the mattress, her eyes wide. She reached up and touched her fingers to her mouth.

He'd been overwhelmed. He'd been grateful. He'd gotten caught up in the moment, she'd replied. And all of those were fine justifications given the highly charged nature of the news he'd broken to his parents.

So what the hell was *her* excuse? And why was she feeling so darn disappointed?

Something was wrong with Michael. For the past two days he seemed extremely preoccupied. Oh, he still arrived home at the same time. He still spent time with Hailey. But he was distant, and obviously had something on his mind.

Sophia couldn't help but wonder if the kiss they had shared might have anything to do with his pensiveness.

Although she wasn't an obnoxiously confrontational person, neither was she one to fret over the unknown. What better way to discover what was going on than to ask him outright?

After feeding and changing Hailey, Sophia took the baby to Michael's office.

The door was open and he had his back to her. He was bent over an open drawer of the filing cabinet, searching through some paperwork.

She knocked. "Hailey's ready for bed. I thought you might want to say good-night."

The strain on Michael's face immediately eased when he gazed upon his daughter. "I'd like to do more than that," he said. He dropped the file on his desk top, came toward them and scooped Hailey into his arms. After planting a kiss on her creamy forehead, he said, "I think I'll tuck her in, if you don't mind."

"You're the daddy. I don't mind at all." He turned to go and she said, "But, Michael, when you're finished, would you have time to talk?"

"Sure," he said. "What's up? Is everything okay with Hailey?"

"Everything is fine. She's eating well and growing more beautiful every day."

He grinned in agreement with her last statement, and Sophia felt an odd hitch in her chest. The man was clearly taken with his baby girl, and Sophia was amazed to find that terribly appealing.

"She is beautiful, isn't she?" Without awaiting an answer, he said, "This won't take too long. We can talk in the living room."

She nodded.

About fifteen minutes later, she heard him close the

door of the nursery. He came into the living room and went straight to the liquor cabinet.

"Would you like a drink?" he asked. He poured himself a scotch.

"Wine would be nice, thanks. Hailey's still taking both a morning nap and an afternoon nap, so I can't complain of needing to unwind."

It took him a minute or two to uncork the bottle. He filled a glass and brought it to her where she sat on the couch. "Still, being on call so many hours during the day and night," he said, "you deserve to relax a little."

She sipped, the merlot leaving behind a spicy after-taste on her tongue. "This is good. Thanks."

"You're welcome." He eased himself down into the chair. "So what was it you wanted to talk about?"

The stem of the crystal wineglass felt smooth in her fingers. "I want to know if you're upset with me. Because of what happened…you know, in the hallway a couple of nights ago."

"Upset with you? Of course not. You didn't do anything."

The surprise expressed on his face and in his tone was instant and unmitigated confirmation that whatever it was that had engrossed his thoughts for the last two days, it wasn't her. Or the kiss they had shared.

She felt a little let down.

"That's good," she said, hiding the fact that she felt the exact opposite. What did he mean she hadn't done anything? She'd reacted to his kiss. She'd kissed him back. How could he not be upset about that?

But she didn't dare release those thoughts. What had happened between them should never happen between people who had a business arrangement.

Instead, she said, "You've been awfully quiet ever since…that night that we…you know…"

"The night we kissed," he supplied.

She nodded.

He shifted in the chair. "If I'm to be entirely honest, I have to clarify. The night *I* kissed *you*." He grimaced. "I pretty much attacked you. And I'm sorry about that, Sophia."

Darn it! She hadn't wanted to hear him apologize. But there it was. Right out in the open.

She took a drink from her glass. Oh, well, she thought. She might not have wanted to hear that he regretted kissing her, but it was what she needed to hear. It was what was best for her life plan. She couldn't deny that. Besides, intimate behavior between business associates was strictly forbidden.

"I have been preoccupied," he explained. "I realized that it was time to organize a party for my employees, to celebrate my top investors. I push them all year, and I like to reward them for all their hard work with a little get-together."

Disappointment flashed through her, sharp and stabbing, when she realized that he really hadn't given those moments in the hall with her a second thought. But she shoved the odd sense of disappointment aside. What else could she expect from a man who professed to have dated more women than he could count? Of course, a swift, tiny kiss would be neither memorable nor important. No matter how knee-melting she had found it.

"They've all been asking about Hailey," he continued, smoothly. "So I thought I might have all of them over here. Have some catered food brought in and hire someone to tend bar. But I don't have a clue where to begin."

"Don't you have a secretary or an assistant to help you with something like that?"

He swallowed the last of the amber liquid in his highball glass. "My secretary has informed me that party planning is not in her job description." His jaw went tight. "And I no longer have an assistant."

He gazed across the room, and almost as if speaking to himself, he muttered, "I know there was a file with information on the businesses we use for these things. Catering, table and linen rentals, florists. I can't believe she'd—" Ice glittered in his dark eyes. "Yes, I can believe she would."

"Who's she?" Sophia asked, shaking her head in confusion. "And what is it you can believe she'd do?"

Michael got up, went to the bar and poured himself another drink. He turned and leaned the small of his back against the cabinet. "Ray Anne," he said.

Sophia sat up straighter. "*Hailey's mother was your assistant*?" She couldn't restrain her surprise.

"Please don't call her that." Michael swiped his hand over his jaw. "She might have given birth to my daughter, but the woman is not, and will never be, Hailey's mother."

So Ray Anne had been Michael's assistant. Interesting. Sophia never imagined the woman who deceived Michael would end up being someone in his employ.

Not knowing what to say, she remained silent.

"I know Ray Anne kept meticulous records on this kind of thing." He tipped his glass and swallowed. "But it would be just like her to steal or destroy the damn files just to throw a monkey wrench into the spokes of my life."

Sophia said, "Listen, this isn't something to get all bent out of shape over. Once, my assistant Karen cleaned out my files. She thought she was doing me a favor." Her mouth twisted ironically. "Needless to say, it was a favor I could have lived without. I retrieved the names I needed by going over my accounting books. I keep detailed records of the money that flows in and out of The Nanny Place. I'm sure you do the same. Your canceled checks and credit card statements for this time last year will show the names of the companies you hired for your annual party, right?"

"Of course. Thanks." He heaved a sigh. "I should have thought of that on my own. I guess I got too hung up on the discovery that Ray Anne had screwed me over once again."

His harsh choice of verb phrase wasn't lost on her.

"It burns me up that I didn't realize she was too young and too gorgeous for her own good. I should have seen that she was damn conniving."

"Hindsight is an amazing thing," Sophia quipped, hoping her joke would help him to cool off. "History is always clear as crystal. If you allow yourself to continue to dwell on her and what she did, then she's going to be intruding into your life again and again. You can succeed without her records. And I'll help you."

He looked so surprised by her offer that she laughed.

"But you're busy with Hailey."

"I told you, she sleeps for hours every day," she said. "I'll need some information—how many people you expect, what you want to serve, oh, and you'll have to find the names of the entertaining services you use. But I'd be happy to send out invitations and make the arrangements."

The cloud of angst that had been hovering over him for two days seemed to dissipate before her very eyes, and the appreciation he felt was obvious. He didn't have to voice it, but he did.

And Sophia flushed with pleasure. She should not get this much enjoyment out of offering to help him make a few party preparations. She put a great deal of effort into studying her merlot before taking a drink in some inane attempt to hide the heat slowly creeping up her neck and into her cheeks.

The next week sailed by swiftly. Michael was in much better spirits when he arrived home each day promptly at five thirty. And Hailey, seeming to sense her daddy's good mood, was sweet as could be.

Each evening, Sophia and Michael spent time talking about the party for his employees. He'd found most of the information they needed in his banking and credit card statements. And he'd provided Sophia with a guest list.

She had to admit, she enjoyed herself around him when he was relaxed. Last night, they'd found themselves laughing so loudly over some of Michael's sillier suggestions for the gathering that they'd awakened Hailey, and Sophia had slipped into the nursery to pat the baby's bottom until she drifted back to sleep.

Because it was Saturday morning, Sophia was preparing to leave Michael's condo for her weekend off.

"You'll be okay?" she asked him.

His spine straightened with confidence, his daughter tucked neatly in the crook of his arm. "I'll be just fine, I think."

"I'm just a phone call away," she reminded him. "Oh, and I left one of my soft fleece pullovers in the nursery. Just in case."

"I saw that when I went to get Hailey this morning. I appreciate your thoughtfulness very much."

"Okay then—" she picked up her jacket "—I guess I'll be off."

"I'll have a date chosen for the party on Monday. I know that's what's holding everything up. It'll have to be soon, though."

She nodded. "As soon as you set a date, I can get everything else rolling."

"I don't know what I'd do without you, Sophia."

Instantly, an intriguing tensity charged the air. Ever since she'd offered to help him make the awards celebration a success, she'd noticed the mysterious energy that hummed around them now vibrated like a live entity.

Something concentrated flashed in his eyes when he looked at her, sparked his voice when he talked to her.

At first, she had to admit, she'd enjoyed it. It made her feel…attractive. It made her feel desirable; and that was hysterical because following Michael's rules forced her to keep herself pretty dowdy. But it was very clear that he'd begun looking at her through different eyes, seeing her in a different light than he had when she'd first arrived. And the idea that an intelligent and successful—not to mention handsome—man like Michael would find her appealing was a real stroke to her ego. She was only too happy to lend a hand to make his party a success. The fact that he stared so intently at her, sought her opinion on this party detail or that one, was just an added bonus. A secret thrill.

However, the energy thrumming between them seemed to be growing more and more potent, and she was beginning to perceive something. A warning? Danger? Not in any physical sense, of course…but definitely in an emotional sense. This invisible current was making her very uneasy.

Just when the awkwardness was swelling to a level of true discomfort, the front doorbell rang.

"Who could *that* be so early?" he murmured.

When he went to the door and opened it, there was quite a commotion as an elderly couple swooped in to greet Michael with hugs and kisses. It was easy for Sophia to guess that Michael's parents had come for a visit, and she was relieved that she'd stayed in the living room so that the happy group could have a small margin of privacy.

"We considered flying," the elderly man said to Michael, "but decided we didn't mind driving."

"We've been on the road since the morning after you called." Excitement fairly rang in the woman's tone. "We arrived so late last night that we decided to wait until this morning to come banging on your door. I brought pastries from Cannon's."

The bakery, located on the outskirts of the city, had a great reputation.

"Aw, Mom, Dad," Michael groaned, "I'm sorry that your trip's been interrupted."

"Nonsense," his mother said, handing the white bag she'd been carrying to her husband and slipping out of her jacket. "This is our first and only grandchild we're talking about." She fluttered her hands, excitement dancing in her eyes. "Here. Gimme, gimme!"

Michael handed Hailey over to her grandmother.

"Oh, my," the woman crooned, "you're gorgeous, Hailey. Absolutely adorable. Isn't she, Bradley?"

"She sure is," his father said. "And has our Hailey got ten fingers and ten toes?"

Chuckling, Michael watched them take a detailed assessment. He beamed. "She's darned near perfect."

"I wouldn't expect anything else." His dad grinned wide. "I know I said it on the phone, but I have to say it again. Congratulations, son."

"Thanks, Dad."

There was another round of hugs, and then Michael turned to face Sophia. "Come inside," he told his parents. "There's someone here I'd like you to meet."

Once they were all in the living room, he made the introductions.

"Mom, Dad, this is Sophia."

"So this is the nanny." The woman offered an open smile. "The woman you told us about?"

"The very one," Michael said.

Michael's mother studied Sophia for an instant and murmured, "She *is* beautiful."

There was no way for Sophia to know if this was merely a very nice compliment being voiced, or if the woman was agreeing with a comment Michael had made during their conversation days ago. She offered a pleasant nod of thanks, but inside she felt extremely discombobulated.

Michael completed the introductions. "Sophia these are my parents—Sylvia and Bradley Taylor."

"Mrs. Taylor. Mr. Taylor." Sophia reached out her hand. "It's nice to meet you."

"Oh, we can't have all this formal stuff. Makes me un-comfortable." Mr. Taylor chuckled and he enveloped her in a warm bear hug. "We're just regular Joes, no matter how uptown my son has become with all this leather and chrome fanciness. You call me Bradley, you hear?"

"And I'm Sylvia." Because she held the baby,

Michael's mother didn't hug her, but she did press a warm palm to Sophia's cheek.

Sophia's smile spread wide, deciding immediately that she liked these friendly, down-to-earth people. "I certainly don't want either of you feeling uncomfortable around the likes of me. I'm a regular Joe, myself."

"Michael told us you've been a lifesaver for him," Sylvia said. "I want to thank you for taking such good care of our brand-new granddaughter." She tossed a gaze at Michael. "And our son."

Thinking about the raving bull Michael had been in her office not all that long ago, Sophia nearly laughed. He certainly wouldn't have called her a lifesaver then, she was sure.

"You're very welcome," Sophia said. "But all I did was speed up the new dad's learning process. He'd have learned it all eventually. Babies have a knack for teaching us what we need to know."

Sylvia gazed down at the baby. "Isn't that the truth? When Michael was born—"

"Okay, okay," Michael broke into the women's conversation, "I'd prefer you leave out stories about my babyhood for now, if you don't mind." He moved closer. "Besides, Sophia was just leaving."

"Leaving?" Sylvia's smile waned.

"Aw," Michael's father said. "But we just arrived."

"And I'm happy you're here," Michael told them. "But Sophia has weekends off. She's been working hard all week. And she's got plenty to do, I'm sure. She'll be back Monday morning."

"But we were only planning to stay the weekend," Sylvia complained. "We have to get back on the road on Monday. We have nonrefundable theater tickets in

New York City for Tuesday night." The woman turned to Sophia. "I have a thousand questions about Hailey. And I just know Michael won't be able to answer a single one of them. Could you stay long enough to have a cup of coffee and a cream tart?"

Michael shook his head. "But, Mom—"

"It's okay," Sophia told him. "I don't mind staying for breakfast."

As it turned out, one cup of coffee turned into two, and Sophia truly enjoyed the hour and a half she spent sitting around the kitchen table, chatting with Sylvia, Bradley and Michael, and nibbling on the delicious pastries. They were all like one big, happy family. Michael played his role as Daddy to perfection, heating up Hailey's bottle so his mother could feed her and then taking his daughter to the nursery for a diaper change.

When Sophia was alone with Michael's parents, Sylvia commented, "He seems so good with her."

"He's an excellent father," Sophia said. "Very loving. Very concerned."

"We thought he'd never settle down," Bradley said. "We thought we'd never have a grandbaby."

"That's true." Sylvia smoothed her finger over the handle of the spoon sitting next to her coffee cup. "That's why we were absolutely astounded when he told us about Hailey. We were ecstatic."

The woman's elation was apparent in the moisture glittering in her eyes.

"We have our granddaughter," Bradley quipped lightly. "Now all we need is for our son to round out his little family."

The older couple looked at each other, their gleaming gazes locked, and Sophia got the strange sense that they were in the midst of some kind of silent conversation. She thought that was nice; to have someone with whom you were so close that you could almost communicate without speaking a single word.

Bradley and Sylvia wanted Michael to find a wife. Someone to complete his family unit. Sophia guessed that was a very normal wish for any parent to have for his or her child.

Then she wondered about her own mother. Had her mom ever yearned for grandchildren? If she had, she'd never said. Had her mom ever wished that Sophia and her brother would find lifelong mates, someone to spend their lives with? Once again, Sophia had to admit that her mother had never spoken on the topic. Her mom had rammed home to both her children the importance of educating themselves so that they'd have the knowledge and skills to support themselves.

A deep sadness swathed Sophia in a profound heaviness. She knew her mother had harped so only because she hadn't wanted her children to have to work their fingers to nubs in myriad menial jobs as she'd had to do in order to pay the rent on their tiny efficiency apartment, to clothe and feed her kids…to simply survive.

"So what do you say?" Bradley asked.

The query shook Sophia out of the dreary past, and she felt momentarily flustered by what she'd obviously missed.

"I know we have to let you go for now." Sylvia's smile was open and warm. "But we'd love for you to have dinner with us tonight. Along with Michael and Hailey, too, of course."

"Oh, b-but," Sophia blubbered, "I don't think I should intrude on your time with Michael and the baby."

"Nonsense." Michael entered the kitchen, handing his freshly changed daughter to his mother. "I'd love for you to have dinner with us."

Sophia blinked. "You would?" Fearing that she was going to blush, she blurted, "Okay, then. I'd love to go." She stood. "I should be going. I have a thousand things to do. Until this evening, then." She nodded goodbye to everyone.

"Wait," Michael said. "I'll walk you to the door."

When they reached the foyer, Michael slid his hand over Sophia's forearm. "Thanks for being so nice to my parents."

"I had a great time this morning," she told him. "They're wonderful people." She shot him a mischievous grin and whispered, "But I should warn you, they're looking to marry you off."

He chuckled softly. "Oh, that's something they've been trying to do for years now."

She nodded. "Just so you know."

His gaze warmed. "Thanks for the warning."

At that moment, something balmy and wonderful passed between them. Sophia was at a loss to figure out exactly what it was.

She opened the door. "I'll see you later, then."

Finally, he pulled his hand back, let it fall to his side. "I'll call you this afternoon with the details."

"Sounds good."

Sophia felt as if she were floating down the hall. A gray qualm hovered at the edge of her thoughts, though, and she knew it was just waiting to swoop in and ruin this divine lightness that filled her. She closed off the

shadowy foreboding—shut it off like a leaky faucet.
She stepped into the elevator and pushed the button that
would take her to the building's foyer, basking in the
sunny joy that lifted her heart.

Chapter Six

Sophia arranged to meet Michael, Hailey, Sylvia and Bradley at The Steakhouse Grill on Union Street. The restaurant had just recently opened in the city and had earned rave reviews in area newspapers. The atmosphere was casual, so Sophia fit right in when she pushed her way through the door wearing black leather boots, low-waist dark denims, a wide black belt and a burnt orange rib-knit turtleneck sweater.

Because she wasn't "on the clock," she felt free to coat her eyelashes with mascara and highlight her cheekbones with a little blush. Tinted gloss had her lips glistening. She'd never been one to wear loads of makeup, but accentuating her best features always made her feel good about herself. She'd curled the ends of her hair and let it fall loose around her shoulders.

She told the hostess she was with the Taylor party, and the teen escorted her through the busy establishment. The sound of clattering cutlery mingled with the buzz of dozens of conversations while the smoky scent of grilling beef hung heavy in the air. Sophia inhaled deeply and realized she was hungry.

Turning a corner in the main dining room, her gaze homed in on Michael immediately. He was laughing at something one of his parents had said. He looked relaxed, and devilishly sexy.

She'd floated around all day, revisiting the heated closeness she and Michael had shared before she'd left his condo. Even Karen had noticed the change in her when she'd stopped by to pick up Flicker. Her assistant had commented that Sophia was beaming and had poked and prodded for the cause. Sophia had sidestepped her efforts and had told Karen that she was merely enjoying her weekend off. She hadn't told her assistant that she was having dinner with Michael and his family, and she wasn't quite sure why, really.

When there were still five yards between her and the table, Michael chanced to glance up. And their gazes locked. His laughter faded as he studied her from the top of her head to the tips of her booted toes.

He pulled the crimson linen napkin from his lap and stood when she reached him. "Hello," he murmured.

She greeted him with a grin. "Hi. I'm not late, am I?" She knew she was right on time. But her heart was beating too fast, and her thoughts seemed to race through her head at alarming speed. She smiled at Bradley and Sylvia. "How is everyone? Enjoying your visit?"

"Very much," Bradley said as Sophia slid into the empty chair waiting for her.

She was keenly aware that Michael eased back

down into his chair and dropped his linen napkin across his thighs.

"We didn't leave the house all day." Sylvia set down her glass of water. "And that was fine with us. All we wanted to do was catch up with Michael and get acquainted with our grandbaby. We've had a wonderful visit."

Hailey's carrier was tucked between the proud grandparents.

"I see our baby girl is snoozing again," Sophia said. "She certainly is a good baby, isn't she?"

Both Sylvia and Bradley agreed, pure delight lighting their expressions.

"How about you?" Michael asked. "How was your day?"

Sophia swiveled her head to see his attention was focused on her. "It was very productive, thanks. I stopped in to chat with my assistant and pick up my cat. As usual, Karen is doing a bang-up job of running the office."

"The office?" Sylvia asked.

"Sophia is the owner of The Nanny Place," Michael told his mother. "Her usual job is placing nannies, not acting as one. But—"

He stopped suddenly, and Sophia suppressed the smile threatening to curl the corners of her lips, curious about how he would explain her presence in his home.

Immediately, he seemed to realize he'd backed himself into a corner. He looked apologetic.

"Well, you see," he started slowly, "I had a little trouble with the nannies she sent me."

"Fired three of them, he did." Sophia rested her elbows on the table and laced her fingers together. "Three highly trained young women, I might add."

Bradley looked stunned and Sylvia's jaw went slack.

"Michael," his mother chastised.

Sophia chuckled at his discomfort. "It was all due to new-daddy jitters, I believe. I think he felt that no one could do a good job of taking care of his precious princess."

"That much is true," he mumbled, offering her a quick wink. He told his parents, "So Sophia offered to come to the house for a while to assure me that I could count on her and The Nanny Place to take good care of Hailey. And she's done just that. She's working on finding an older, more experienced woman to take care of Hailey."

Not wanting to make matters worse for him with his parents, Sophia decided not to bring up the fact that she felt forced into this position because he'd threatened to spread around his poor opinion of her business. Now that she looked back on the whole matter, it seemed comical, but it certainly hadn't while it was happening.

The waitress arrived to take their orders, and since the brand-new restaurant was known for its spectacular steaks, that's what they all requested, along with sides of house salad, buttery baked potatoes and hot rolls.

While they waited for dinner to be served, Michael's parents told Sophia about some of their adventures on the extended excursion they had dubbed the Great USA Road Trip.

"I loved the Dakotas," Sylvia said.

"Mount Rushmore was amazing," Bradley said. "Did you know it took fourteen years to complete?"

Before Sophia could respond, Sylvia said, "And the Crazy Horse Memorial. Of course, it's not finished, but when it is, it'll be spectacular."

"And we visited Jewel Cave." Bradley reached out and covered his wife's hand with his. "One hundred thirty miles of passages. Can you imagine?"

LAS VEGAS
GAME

▼ DETACH AND MAIL CARD TODAY! ▼

Just scratch off the gold box with a coin. Then check below to see the gifts you get!

YES! I have scratched off the gold box. Please send me my **2 FREE BOOKS** and **gift for which I qualify.** I understand that I am under no obligation to purchase any books as explained on the back of this card.

310 SDL EFXZ   310 SDL EFWQ

FIRST NAME   LAST NAME

ADDRESS

APT.#   CITY

(S-R-08/06)

STATE/PROV.   ZIP/POSTAL CODE

7	7	7

Worth TWO FREE BOOKS
plus a BONUS Mystery Gift!

Worth TWO FREE BOOKS!

TRY AGAIN!

www.eHarlequin.com

Offer limited to one per household and not valid to current Silhouette Romance® subscribers. All orders subject to approval.

BUSINESS REPLY MAIL

FIRST-CLASS MAIL   PERMIT NO. 717-003   BUFFALO, NY

POSTAGE WILL BE PAID BY ADDRESSEE

SILHOUETTE READER SERVICE
3010 WALDEN AVE
PO BOX 1867
BUFFALO NY 14240-9952

NO POSTAGE
NECESSARY
IF MAILED
IN THE
UNITED STATES

"We only saw a fraction of them. And Wind Cave with that rare formation. What was it called, honey?" Sylvia asked. "Boxwork, wasn't it?"

Her husband nodded. "And further north, Devil's Lake was very peaceful. Just beautiful."

"We loved it so much, we camped there nearly a week," Sylvia said.

They told of riding in the Gateway Arch in St. Louis, Missouri; of stepping back into the Victorian era while touring Mackinac Island in Michigan; of dancing the night away in Chicago's hottest nightspots.

They mentioned the redwoods in Washington, the Japanese Garden in Portland, Oregon, and Tess, the fifty-foot woman with visible organs in the California Science Center. It was clear that they sought out both nationally known attractions as well as more obscure ones. Sophia thought it all sounded like fun.

Even after the food arrived, the Great USA Road Trip dominated the conversation. But Sophia didn't mind at all. It was clear that Michael's parents were truly enjoying driving all over North America, searching out wonderful things to see and experience, and apparently they still had plenty of exciting destinations they had yet to visit.

The waitress came and cleared their table. And then she returned to take their dessert order.

"I'll have a slice of apple pie and cup of decaf coffee," Sylvia said.

Hailey stirred, and Bradley leaned over his granddaughter. "Well, look who's decided to wake up."

The waitress looked at Sophia. "I'll have apple pie and coffee, too. Thanks."

The baby became cranky. Not crying, just fussing.

"She probably needs a dry diaper." Michael made to rise, but his mother beat him to it.

"You sit," Sylvia said. "Let me do it." She glanced down, then looked under the table. "Oh, Michael. You told me to grab the diaper bag on the way out of the house. I got busy talking to your father and I forgot."

"Maybe we just left it in the car," Michael suggested.

The woman shook her head. "I specifically remember only picking up my purse."

Michael whipped the napkin off his lap. "That's no problem. We'll just cancel dessert and go on home. Do you mind, Sophia?"

"Of course not. I understand." Absently, she picked up her own napkin and set it on the table.

"I feel awful," Sylvia said. "This is all my fault." Her eyes lit suddenly. "I know. Bradley and I will take Hailey home. You two stay and finish your dinner. I'd hate to be the one who made you miss dessert."

"But, Mom—"

"I insist." Excitement fairly glowed from the older woman. "Besides, it will give me and your father a chance to say we babysat our grandbaby. Every grandparent needs those bragging rights, don't you know?"

Immediately caught in the whirlwind of his wife's enthusiasm, Bradley got up from the table. "Sylvia's absolutely right. We need some alone time with Hailey. Sophia, could you drive Michael back to his place after you've finished your pie and coffee?"

A quick glace at Michael told Sophia that he felt completely bowled over by his parents' unexpected suggestion. Well, she felt the same way.

"B-but, I didn't drive," she stammered. "I live right off Delaware Avenue, so I walked."

"That's an even better reason for us to leave Michael with you," Sylvia said. "It's grown dark. It's not safe for a woman to be walking the streets alone."

That was downright silly, and Sophia knew it. She felt perfectly safe in her city. Clearly, Sylvia was jumping for reasons to take Hailey home on her own. Sophia thought it would have been touching had she not been so overwhelmed by the flurry of this swiftly turning tide.

Alone with Michael? Without Hailey between them, what on earth would they talk about?

The waitress stood nearby, silent and patient.

"Michael can walk you home, Sophia," Bradley proposed, "and then you can drive him back to his place." He looked at his son. "Or you could take a cab, Michael. Or…or you could call me and I'll come get you." He picked up his jacket. "Any way you want to work it out is okay with us."

Bradley helped his wife into her jacket, and then slid Hailey and her baby carrier closer to him.

The surprise Michael had been feeling was now dissolving to humor. He was grinning when he looked at Sophia. Softly, he said, "I think my parents really, *really* want a chance to be alone with Hailey."

Sophia didn't know what to say. She was sure that her smile must look plastic and forced. It sure felt that way.

"Do you mind?" he asked her.

Did she mind? Of course, she minded. Being alone with him was going to be awkward.

"I don't mind at all," she lied, astounded by the words that slipped from her lips with such ease.

A few more seconds of chaos ensued as Michael handed over the keys to his car and went over detailed instructions concerning the latch on the baby's car seat.

Finally, Sylvia and Bradley said their goodbyes, and then hustled out of the restaurant thoroughly steeped in the thrill of having the baby all to themselves.

Michael shook his head and heaved a sigh. "They're nuts, my parents."

"Maybe just a little," Sophia quipped. "But it's a nice kind of nuts."

They laughed; however, she still battled the pensiveness that tensed her stomach.

The waitress approached the table. "So, ma'am, do you still want the apple pie and coffee?"

"Yes, thanks," she told the girl.

"And for you sir?"

"I'll have the same," Michael said. "And I'm sorry about the ruckus."

"Oh, that's no problem, sir." The waitress beamed. "I'll be right back with your order."

Once they were alone, Michael turned to Sophia, directing every nuance of his attention on her.

"Thanks for being such a good sport about all this," he said.

"I don't mind. Really."

He chuckled, and Sophia loved the sound.

"I've decided that you're a giver," he told her.

Uncertain about what he meant exactly, she remained silent.

"Since meeting you," he continued, "I've said 'thank you' much more often than I'm used to. You like to see people happy, so you give. You've sure given me a great deal over the past week and a half." He lifted one shoulder. "Sure, you started off giving me exactly what I demanded in order to see that I was a satisfied client. But you went above and beyond what could ever be expected. You gave me advice about my daughter. You educated me about the needs of babies. And then you offered to help me pull my party together. You've been great to my parents. Answering all their questions about Hailey." He nodded. "You're a giver, all right."

He'd gifted her with a lovely compliment. One that she accepted with a quiet smile of sincere gratitude.

The waitress brought a tray laden with coffee cups and saucers, cream and two thick slabs of warm apple pie.

Sophia inhaled the scent of cinnamon. "Mmmmm," she said, closing her eyes in order to fully enjoy it.

"Does smell good," Michael murmured.

Glancing at him, she realized that he hadn't taken his gaze off her and heat tightened her belly.

Although she'd dreaded the idea of being alone with him, it turned out that they were able to find quite a bit to talk about. They discussed Michael's parents and the love-at-first-sight relationship that had sprouted between them and Hailey. Then the conversation turned to the party and they hammered out more details. But not a second passed that Sophia wasn't aware of the allure humming around them.

Soon the last of the coffee was gone, and all that was left on their plates were a few crumbs of pie crust. Michael paid the bill, and then the two of them went out onto the sidewalk.

"It's a nice night," she commented, looking up at the clear, starry sky.

"Yeah," he agreed. He laughed softly. "We don't get out very often at night, do we?"

"Hailey goes to bed early and wakes up early. We have to live by her schedule for the time being." She took a few steps in silence, then said, "Babies have command of their parents' lives for such a short time, though. Living by her schedule isn't all that tough, is it?"

"Absolutely not. I wouldn't want it any other way."

"Whoa, now," she said laughing, "be careful there. Once she's a teenager and she's staying up all hours of the night…"

"Ah, yes. I see what you mean."

His willingness to agree with her made her want to tease him. "You've changed so much," she said. "You've made a complete turnaround. You've mellowed into a big softie. When I first came to work for you, you argued with everything I said."

Humor made his eyes twinkle merrily. "I could say the same about you. You were the queen of quarrelling."

She grinned. "True. But it was for a good cause."

"The best," he said, his voice velvet soft. "I'm learning that I'll do anything for my daughter. Even to the point of shutting up and listening. And learning." He absently fingered the button on his cuff. "I just wish the other nannies had taken the time to explain—"

Her chuckle cut short his comment and he eyed her curiously.

"Michael, you can't be serious. They were too intimidated to say a word."

"Intimidated?" His step halted and he blinked. "By *me*?"

She just shook her head. He had the good grace to laugh, and she joined him.

They both fell quiet then and walked half a block. Sophia couldn't help but notice that the silence was just as easy as the conversation had been during dessert. It was a pleasant surprise.

They met a woman carrying two bags of groceries, and then a young couple holding hands, their heads bent close as if they didn't want another living soul to overhear their shared secrets. Three teens on skateboards came up from behind to pass them, two of them vaulting their boards off the curb and out into the street in order to avoid them.

Finally, Michael asked, "How did The Nanny Place come about?"

Sophia had to smile. "If anyone would have told me that I'd actually become an entrepreneur when I was attending college, I'd never have believed it."

He looked intrigued. "What had you planned to be when you grew up?"

"I majored in child psychology," she told him. "I seriously thought I'd become a child advocate in some capacity. A social worker." She shrugged. "School counselor, maybe. A therapist. But so many people warned me that people who go into social work often burn out after just a few years, so I started taking business classes, too. Ended up graduating with a double major, in fact. I'm kind of proud of that."

She could tell from his expression that he agreed that her achievement was something to be proud of. That pleased her.

"Where'd you go to school?" he asked.

"Lehigh University. I grew up in Allentown, which is very close to Lehigh." She inhaled the distinctive scent of boxwood as they passed a tall, neatly manicured hedge. "I was able to live at home with my mom and save a little money by not having to fork out room and board at school."

"So what happened to your plans of going into social work?"

Sophia carefully avoided a rough, unleveled spot on the sidewalk. "I have a friend who wasn't interested in college. Tracy worked various jobs, and then found an ad for nanny school. She attended, and it took her six months to earn her certificate. I was surprised by how thoroughly she was trained.

"Anyway, the year that I was a senior at Lehigh, Tracy found a nanny position here in Wilmington." Sophia lifted her hand, palm up. "But the family was forced to relocate unexpectedly, and Tracy didn't want to move. So she needed to find another job. And she had to find one fast in order to keep paying her car payment."

They turned onto Delaware Avenue. "What she found was that there were nannies, lots of them, in the same boat she was in. Many parents were reluctant, for one reason or another, to advertise their need for child care in the local paper. I got the idea of a nanny placement service. As soon as I graduated, I checked it out. Philadelphia already has two such services, whereas Wilmington didn't have one at all. So I moved here."

"Smart woman," he murmured. "Why compete when you can go where there is no competition?"

"My thought, exactly." Sophia noticed suddenly that he'd moved closer to her. His arm brushed hers with nearly every step. She was very conscious of the heat of him, the subtle scent of his cologne. Her thoughts speeded up considerably and she had to focus in order not to lose track of the conversation.

"Business was slow, at first," she admitted. "I had to wait until people found my advertisements. I placed ads in the local papers and in *Delaware Today* magazine. But the magazine is only published once a month." She grinned. "I went door-to-door in the more upscale neighborhoods, but I quickly discovered people do not like face-to-face solicitations."

He laughed. "Yeah, it's sort of like telemarketers calling at dinnertime. People don't want to be bothered in the comfort of their own home."

She bobbed her head animatedly. "That's when I started doing mass mailings. It was a lot of work, of course, discerning the addresses of possible clients, but well worth it in the end. People began to respond. They came seeking my help, and due to word of mouth, my business took off."

"That word of mouth is a good business concept," he said. "It pulls in clients in my line of business, too."

She eyed him ironically. "So I guess you know how important it was to me to make you happy and save my good business reputation."

He looked chagrined. "Now, Sophia…I seriously doubt I'd have followed through on my threat."

Stopping in her tracks, she plunked her fist on her hip. "You are lying through your teeth, mister. You'd have complained to anyone who would have listened. You'd have spelled my name frontwards and backwards, if they'd asked you to. I have no doubt. If I've learned nothing else, it's that you're a man of your word."

He had the good sense to avert her gaze. "Yeah," he finally admitted, his head bobbing, "I probably would have. But only because I didn't realize I was a big part of the nightmare. Me and my infamous list of rules."

Sophia found it in her to chuckle. "It *is* comical now, isn't it?"

He shook his head, evidently uncertain. "I don't know that I ever find my own ignorance funny, Sophia."

He struggled against the humor of it for a moment, but then his dark gaze lit and he laughed—albeit ruefully— right along with her.

She guided them down a narrow, tree-lined side street. The leaves on the sycamores had turned red and looked rusty in the yellowy light of the streetlamps.

"This is me," she said, pointing to the brick building on the corner.

The mansion was big enough to have been converted into sixteen separate apartments.

"This is nice," Michael said. "I like the porch."

"It's lovely and shady in the summer," she told him, "but unfortunately everyone who lives here seems too busy to use it."

"That's a shame."

"Well, let me run up and get my car keys and I'll drive you—"

"That's okay," he said. "It's so nice out tonight, I think I'll walk. I only need to cross the bridge and cut across the park. That'll give Mom and Dad a chance to spend more time with Hailey."

She smiled. "Good idea. Listen, Michael, I had a wonderful time tonight. Your folks are great. It was nice. Thank you."

"You're welcome," he said. "I had a good time, too."

At that instant, the easy rapport that they'd enjoyed during dinner and on the walk to her apartment seemed to slowly dissolve away. The strange thing was, it seemed to leave behind dozens of invisible prickly thorns. Sophia swallowed, a vast lump of apprehension gathering in her stomach.

"Well, then," she said, "I guess I should say good-night. I'll see you Monday morning."

He tucked his hands into his trouser pockets, nodding. "'Night."

She was already on the porch, her key in the lock of the front door when he called out to her.

"Change your mind?" she asked, turning to face him. "You want a ride?"

"No." He looked nervous. "But I would like to talk. If you don't mind."

"Sure." Curiosity had Sophia frowning. They'd had the whole walk home to talk. "You want to go inside?"

He shook his head. "Let's just sit out here. Is it too chilly for you?"

"I'm fine." She tucked her keys back into her purse and moved toward the Adirondack chairs positioned on the porch. "But you've turned so serious. You've got me worried. What is it, Michael?"

She sat down on the wooden seat, but he remained standing.

"I've been doing some thinking," he began. He paced three steps, then turned and paced back. "Remember last week? When I—" he laced his fingers, then just as quickly unlaced them "—kissed you?"

What a silly question, she thought. She'd known in her heart that she should have been doing everything in her power to forget. But her subconscious continued to stir up the most sensuous images during the deepest part of the night when she was asleep and most vulnerable, and she awoke almost every morning realizing all over again just how overwhelmed she'd been by his kiss.

"I remember." Surely the tightness in her voice conveyed her opinion that nothing good could come out of what had happened between them.

Again, he paced three steps east, then three steps

west. "I thought it was…nice." Quickly, he amended, "No, it was more than nice. I—I enjoyed it."

"You did?" Her heart thudded. "But I thought you hadn't given it a second thought."

"If I gave you that impression, I certainly didn't mean to. I liked it. I liked it a lot." He went back to pacing. "I was wondering if maybe you did, too. Of course, you probably didn't like it as much as I did. But I was still wondering if maybe you might have enjoyed it…a little, anyway."

His phrasing was schoolboy awkward, and he seemed so ill at ease that, had she not been feeling so unnerved, she'd have thought it was cute.

Without waiting for her to respond, he said, "We seem to get along really well. Now that we're on the same page about Hailey, that is. You're intelligent. You're funny. You've got a great personality. I enjoy being with you, Sophia."

She watched him tread back and forth across the porch. If she hadn't been so taken aback by the subject matter, she'd have thought it quite funny that, so far, he hadn't looked at her once.

He paused, and she got the sense he was preparing himself for some sort of grand finale. Her pulse skittered in some sort of odd triple beat.

His dark eyes converged on her finally, the intensity reflected in them so powerful it stole Sophia's breath away.

"What I'm trying to say," he told her, "is that I find you attractive, Sophia. Very much so. And that I'm interested in…pursuing a…friendship." He spread his palms. "You know. A relationship. Between you and me. Us."

She stared at him for several long moments.

"Michael," she began. Then she stopped. She gazed

off as she fought the panic rising in her chest. She certainly didn't want to hurt his feelings, but she knew all the way down to the marrow of her bones that what he was suggesting was wrong.

She offered him a small, gracious smile, one that was meant to soften an oncoming blow. She kept her tone soft and reassuring. "I'd be lying if I said I don't find you attractive. But I need you to know that I'm not interested in a relationship."

"Oh." He tilted his head a fraction. "Are you not interested in a relationship with anyone? Or just not with me?" He rushed to add, "I know I must sound like an idiot. Ticking off your good qualities, and then, well, forcing the issue. I don't normally have to force this kind of—" embarrassment tightened his features "—issue. The chemistry is right, and, well, the relationship usually just happens. But, I thought that…well, with the trouble I've had in the past…it would be better for me to approach things differently. With my eyes wide open. With everyone knowing what everyone else is thinking and…" His dark gaze looked pained as the rest of his thought petered out.

Again, her smile was polite. "I don't think it's wise for us to be involved in any kind of personal relationship, do you? I work for you. You pay me to take care of your daughter."

He refused to meet her gaze.

"I know this arrangement is only temporary." She stood and tugged at the hem of her sweater. "I'm still working on finding you a new nanny. But even then, we'll still be business associates."

He was forced to nod. "That's true, but…"

She shook her head. "No buts. You got involved with

a business associate once and it caused you a great deal of heartache," she felt the need to remind him.

Again, he nodded, keeping his eyes focused somewhere on the opposite side of the porch railing.

"We both know it's wrong to mix business with pleasure. It just doesn't work." She felt the cool metal of the keys in her hand as she walked to the door. The hinges creaked when she pulled open the screen. "Now, I really must say good-night." Luckily, she got her hands on the correct key without fumbling. The dead bolt clunked.

"Sophia," he said.

With one foot already across the threshold, she swiveled her head toward him. She shook her head in a silent no. "It's against the rules, Michael." She softly called out one last, "Good night," before closing the door behind her.

Chapter Seven

Michael shoved back the blankets and got out of bed. It wasn't as if he were sleeping anyway. He'd tossed and turned through most of the night. The hour was so early the sun hadn't even risen above the horizon. The sky was brightening, though, to a dusky pink.

He followed the scent of brewed coffee into the kitchen. "Morning, Mom," he greeted. "You're up early."

She was sitting at the table pouring a little cream into her mug. "I always get excited when we're about to leave on another adventure. Too excited to sleep, I guess."

"This really has been the trip of a lifetime for you and Dad, hasn't it?" He picked up the glass carafe and poured some of the steamy liquid into a mug for himself.

His mother's happiness was evident. "The trip of a lifetime," she told him, "has been this weekend. Hailey is precious, Michael. I'm so pleased that you called us. I'm just ecstatic that we were able to come right away.

I hate that we're leaving so soon, but your father and I would like to come back for a whole week around Christmas, if that's okay with you."

"I'd love that," he told her. "I really would." He took a drink of coffee and then stretched out his neck.

"You look tired. Didn't you sleep well?"

"I'm okay," he lied. There was no need for her to worry about him. He'd get over Sophia's rebuff soon enough, he was sure of it.

"We were so busy shopping yesterday," his mother said, the casual innocence in her tone too sweet to be truly above suspicion, "that I never did get to ask about how you made out having dessert with Sophia Saturday night."

He laughed softly. "What is it about mothers, anyway? Do you have some sort of extrasensory perception?"

She grinned and shrugged. "I can't say. But if we do have any kind of special powers, I'm sure love has something to do with it. We can tell when something's bothering our children."

The room fell silent as both mother and son concentrated on sipping their coffee.

Finally, she quietly prodded him. "She's a lovely girl, that Sophia."

"She is." He did his best to keep his tone as noncommittal as possible.

"And she's really good with Hailey."

This time he only nodded in response. He really didn't want to discuss Sophia with his mother.

A frown furrowed his mom's forehead as she steered the conversation in a completely different direction. "You've explained the situation with Hailey's birth, but are you entirely certain that her mother is out of the picture for good? Is there any chance that the two of you might—"

"No chance." He set the mug on the table. "None. Ray Anne isn't interested in Hailey. She signed over all rights. And the last I heard, she left the state."

His mother shook her head. "For the life of me, I can't understand how a woman can give birth to a baby—become the mother of a beautiful daughter—and just walk away."

Michael absently smoothed his fingertips along the warm ceramic. "But that's not how she viewed Hailey, Mom," he explained. "To her, the baby we created was nothing but a meal ticket."

Clearly, the mere idea sickened the older woman. She whispered, "It's such a coldhearted thing to do." Then she sobered. "Hailey's better off without a woman like that in her life. So are you, son." After pausing, she murmured, "What is this world coming to?"

He had no answer to offer to such a broad and complicated question, so he remained silent.

There was no awkwardness in the quiet that settled between them. Michael had always enjoyed being around his parents. He was comfortable with them. They were good and caring people. He didn't just love them, he liked them. He respected them, too.

That's why he'd been so reluctant to tell them about Hailey, and the dark and underhanded circumstances surrounding her birth.

However, they hadn't judged him. He should have known they wouldn't, should have known that they would offer him nothing but positive support. But he'd been so embarrassed by his own behavior, by his own poor choices, that his logic had been colored. Thank goodness Sophia had talked him into calling his mom and dad.

"She's going to need a mother, you know."

His mom's voice nudged him out of deep thought. He blinked. "You're right."

"You should think about finding a wife."

He suppressed a smile. "You're right. I should think about it."

He nearly chuckled at her pinched look of frustration.

"Aren't you interested in finding that special someone, in getting married?"

His soft laughter echoed in the kitchen. "Mom, I'm dealing with a lot right now. I have a lot on my plate at work. And I have a new baby to take care of, you know. This is all still new to me."

"I understand that. I do. But what I'm trying to tell you is—I'm not just thinking of Hailey. I'd like for you to have what your father and I have."

"I'd love for that to happen. But I have to point out that what you and Dad have is special. It's rarer than you think."

She shifted her weight on the chair, smiling at the compliment. "You need to make time for a private life, Michael. It's important. For you and for Hailey. You'll never know who might be out there waiting for you if you don't try."

"You're right."

Tapping him on the forearm, she groused, "Would you quit agreeing with me. It's irritating."

Michael laughed. "Sorry, Mom. I didn't mean to irritate you. I promise I'll think about everything you've said."

She crossed her legs and swung her foot in short arcs as she studied her mug intently. "That's all I'm asking."

She allowed the span of two heartbeats to pass before softly casually repeating, "Sophia's a lovely girl."

He nearly choked on the coffee he'd sipped. "Mother!" He chuckled, and when she didn't speak, he teased, "Well, are you trying to spell something out for me?"

"No need." Her gaze was bold and steady when she looked him in the eye. "Clearly my inference was strong enough."

"You have no shame."

She grinned. "Not when it comes to the happiness of my son and granddaughter, I don't. So what do you say about the idea?"

He hemmed and hawed, unable to lift his eyes to his mom's face.

"So you *are* attracted to her! I knew it."

His was amazed. He could never keep anything from the woman.

"You don't have to admit it," Sylvia said. "It's written all over your face."

Unable to come up with a response, he kept quiet.

"And she's certainly interested in you."

Although he was normally very much at ease with his mother, he didn't mind confessing that he was feeling suddenly discomfited.

"Oh, don't look so put out." She uncrossed her legs and scooted her chair an inch toward the table. "Your father and I both noticed her behavior at dinner the other night. Sophia hung on your every word."

"Mom, wait." Michael paused long enough to moisten his suddenly dry lips. "You might think Sophia is interested in me. But, believe me, she's not."

His mother offered a disbelieving grin. "And you would know this *how*?"

He sighed. "Because I talked to her about it when I walked her home after dinner this weekend."

An odd expression chased the smile from her face. "I don't understand, Michael. You just came out and asked her if she was interested in you? I don't like to criticize, but that sounds a bit inhibitive to me."

Self-consciousness warmed his neck and jaw. "Give me a little credit, would you? I eased into it. But the bottom line is—"

"No, no, son," Sylvia gently interrupted. "I'd like more information, please. Just how does a man 'ease into' asking a woman if she's interested in him?"

A sudden and very abnormal timidity swept over him. He didn't like the idea of having his technique—his man moves—evaluated by his mother.

"That's kind of personal, Mom," he murmured.

However, her steady stare told him she wasn't going to back down until he revealed his modus operandi.

Michael sighed. "Okay, okay. It went something like this. I told her that I felt that we got along well, that I thought she was a great person, that I found her attractive, that I'd like for the two of us to pursue a relationship…if, of course, she felt the same way about me." He lifted one shoulder. "But she was very quick to tell me she wasn't interested."

His mom shook her head. "Not interested, my foot. I saw the way she was hanging on your every word at dinner. Oh, she's interested, all right."

"But, Mom, she was clear about how she felt. 'It's against the rules' is what she said."

"Of course, she did, Michael." Sylvia almost grumbled the words. "She's a professional business-woman. She's working for you. And the way you attacked her about the whole thing—backed her into a corner like that—"

"I did no such thing."

"How else could she have responded?"

A little more positively? Michael thought, but immediately he remembered that she *had* responded positively. She'd said the attraction he expressed for her was mutual. But then she'd maintained that dating a man she worked for was taboo.

It's against the rules, is how she'd bluntly put it.

Had she been making some kind of point? Had she been meaning to make him realize how obstinate he'd been about his own list of rules early on?

The second the questions entered his head, he dismissed them. Rebuffing him in order to make a point would have been mean. Sophia didn't have a mean bone in her body. Besides, she had never been shy about telling him exactly how she felt about his rules and regulations. No, that hadn't been her motive at all.

"A woman doesn't want to be put in a tight spot, Michael," his mother continued. "A woman wants to be wooed. She wants a little romance."

"Sylvia, dear heart—" Michael's father padded into the room in his robe and slippers, his eyes still bleary with sleep, his hair tousled. "—didn't we promise years ago that we weren't going to stick out noses into our son's private affairs?"

"Well, good morning to you, too," Sylvia greeted her husband, insult obvious in her rod-straight spine. "I'll have you know I was not sticking my nose into anything. I was merely giving my son a little motherly advice."

The dubious look Bradley gave his wife only served to further offend her.

"You worked hard wooing me, Bradley Taylor."

"I certainly did." He walked over and planted a kiss on her cheek. "And you were worth every backbreaking minute of it."

In an instant, the woman relaxed and she smiled at his teasing. "Thank you, dear. Can I get you a cup of coffee?"

Michael watched her mother go to the cabinet for a mug, then he glanced at his father, who offered him a wink. He smiled in return.

Picking up his coffee, Michael took a drink and let his mind wander. Maybe his mom was right. Maybe what Sophia needed was a little romance.

"Good morning, sister of mine! Have time to talk?"

The sound of her brother's voice made Sophia grin. "For you, Joe? You know I do." She glanced at the clock. "But I do have to leave for work in exactly twelve minutes."

Four years her junior, Joe Stanton was just starting his career as an eighth-grade math teacher, and so far he loved his job. Most people thought pubescent teens were something to steer clear of—like a weepy eye infection—but not Joe. He thrived on his daily dealings with those quirky humanoids that were no longer children, yet weren't quite adults. He had a great rapport with his students and the kids seemed as devoted to him as he was to them. Joe's teaching talent was a rare gift.

"Ah, still working for The Beast, I take it," Joe intoned.

"I am. But I've come to the conclusion that his growl is really quite harmless."

"Oh?"

"I've already told you that he's the kind of man

who likes to manage his environment. He's very organized and—"

"A control freak," Joe offered.

Sophia chuckled. "Now don't be mean. He's a nice guy."

"That's funny," Joe teased. "If I remember correctly, it hasn't been that long ago that he was making your life miserable. Something about a bunch of nonsensical rules for his daughter."

She cradled the phone between her shoulder and ear as she dried the tea cup she'd used this morning. "True. But I've come to the conclusion that he came up with all those rules as a way of controlling a situation that scared him witless."

"He was afraid of a tiny baby?"

Sophia tucked the cup into the cabinet and closed the door. "Don't sound so surprised. Not all men are like you with your natural ability where kids are concerned. Some people have to work at it. And we *are* talking about a newborn here. They can seem quite fragile to inexperienced people. And taking care of one isn't as easy as you might think."

"There's no need to get defensive, sis," Joe said softly.

Is that how she'd sounded? She hung the towel neatly on the rack.

"You've certainly changed your tune about the guy," Joe continued, "since the last time we talked."

Sophia turned and rested the small of her back against the edge of the counter. "I guess I have. I didn't know Michael very well, then." She hadn't kissed him, either. "I guess I was too quick to jump to conclusions about him."

"Hmmm. Is that interest I hear in your voice?"

"Absolutely not." The statement might have been a bold-faced lie, but she'd be darned if she'd utter it with anything except firm conviction.

"Wow." Joe laughed. "You really *are* defensive this morning."

"I am no such thing," she snapped.

Her brother only laughed louder.

Because they'd been inseparable growing up, they now shared a close, unbreakable sibling bond. If a couple of weeks went by where they hadn't talked, one or the other would pick up the phone to find out why. Their relationship was so tight that they could read each other like books. If she wanted him to believe her, she'd better lighten up a bit. Breezily, she told him, "I'd never dream of breaking our pact."

Joe went quiet. "I haven't thought about that for years, sis."

Rough upbringings could turn children into adults who were bitter and resentful, or responsible, creative and tremendously practical. Sophia thanked her lucky stars that she and Joe both fit the second category. Life might have presented them with some hard knocks, but neither of them harbored anger about the things that had happened to them.

Their father, a self-employed house painter, had up and walked out of their lives one day with no explanations and no goodbyes. That had been a horrible turning point for all of them. Mary, Sophia's mother, had spent days feeling lost and panicked. When two weeks passed with no sign of her husband, she knew she had to do something or risk losing the tiny apartment they called home. Unskilled and uneducated, Mary had been forced to find not one, but two menial jobs in order to earn enough money to keep a roof over her children's heads, food in their bellies, shoes on their feet and gas in the car. Taking on this unexpected challenge had been terribly stressful for her.

Twelve-year-old Sophia had quickly learned to cook and clean and do the laundry. She'd also become her younger brother's chief caregiver, and because Joe had been like any other ornery adolescent, the task of watching over him often became multifaceted. Sometimes he'd needed a babysitter, sometimes he'd needed a protector and sometimes he'd needed a warden. But he'd always needed someone who loved him. Sophia might have burned a meal, here or there, while her mother was at work, or she might have been less than diligent about the dust bunnies that had taken up residence under their beds, but she'd never once failed to keep a watchful eye on her brother.

Over the years, Sophia and Joe often shared the confusion and sadness they felt over how and why their father had left them. They wondered what they might have done to cause his discontent, to make him stop loving them. As innocent children are wont to do, they blamed themselves. It wasn't until Sophia was in college, taking psychology classes, that she found out how erroneous their thinking had been.

However, guilt and overwhelming responsibility has a way of making a young girl grow up fast. Sophia had felt horrible for her mother. If Mary wasn't working, she was sleeping, and Sophia realized for whom her mother was exhausting herself. She'd done it for her children.

As the days, weeks and years rolled on, Sophia contemplated their situation and formed some hard opinions about life. Men can leave anytime it suits their fancy. And women are left to pick up the pieces alone.

"Having it all" was a fantasy dreamed up by some slick Hollywood scriptwriter. A whimsical idea that led only to want and misery.

Finding success in life, she decided, was all about choices. Family or job. Love or career. The options were, in her mind, completely clear-cut. Attempting to divide herself between raising a family and building a career would be too much of a challenge for anyone. She'd seen it in her own small family.

So she had made a conscious decision long ago—she would forego marriage and children and she'd work for a living. However, Sophia didn't want just any job. Her mother had worked hard as a waitress by day and she'd been part of a crew that cleaned an office building in the evenings. It had been honest work, but it had also been grueling. Sophia wanted something more for herself.

During her freshman year of college, Sophia had voiced this opinion to her brother, an impressionable fourteen-year-old at the time, and, not surprisingly, he had agreed with her. After watching how their mother had struggled through the years, both of the Stanton siblings had made a pact to abandon the idea of happily ever after, and focus instead on educating themselves, on finding and making a success of their chosen occupations. With Sophia in her thriving nanny-placement business and Joe in his second year of teaching, it looked as if both of them were well on their way to doing just that.

Of course, remembering the promise they made to each other never failed to churn up memories of the reason behind it.

"Mom would be proud of you, Joe," Sophia told her brother. She felt the warmth of his smile across the telephone wire.

"Thanks, sis. I appreciate that. She wanted both of us to go to college, and we did. She wanted both of us to find work we had a passion for, and we did that, too." Joe paused for a moment. "I think she'd be proud of both of us, but I think she'd be awed by you."

Nonplussed, Sophia felt her cheeks heat. "What are you talking about?"

"Well, look at you. You're a true success. You saw a need and you filled it. You started a business. All on your own. You're the sole proprietor of The Nanny Place, and your business is growing every month. You took the risk, and now you're reaping the rewards. Mom would be blown away by what you've done."

She thanked her brother for the effusive compliment. Then she grew quiet, contemplative. "You know something, Joe, Mom could have found the same kind of success that you and I have. If she hadn't had children to worry about, she could have made something of herself, too."

"She had a risk-taking spirit, that's for sure," her brother agreed.

They had both seen the extent of their mother's courage when she'd faced the biggest battle of her life—pancreatic cancer. Although she'd fought the disease with every ounce of her strength, she ultimately lost the fight.

"Where do you think you got it from, sis?" He chuckled. "You know what they say...the nut doesn't fall far from the tree."

Sophia grinned. Joe never had a problem prodding her out of a dark mood. "I think what *they* say is, 'the *apple* doesn't fall far from the tree.'"

"Yes, but what do they know, anyway? I know you, sis, and nut fits you much better," he teased. However, then he sobered. "Mom was determined to survive, no matter what. She passed that stubborn determination on to you. You have a bright and shining spirit of independence, just as she did."

After a few more minutes of conversation, Sophia glanced at the clock and was forced to say her goodbyes to Joe, but not before promising to call him soon. As she gathered up her purse, her jacket and car keys, she couldn't help but ponder all the things her brother had said.

She didn't mind admitting that she'd sacrificed to educate herself, that she'd worked hard to make her business a success, but it had all been worth it. It thrilled her to think her mother would have been proud of her.

Yes, it *had* been worth it. And she wasn't going to toss all that she'd worked for into the wind just because Michael had shown interest in her.

Sure, she was flattered. Sure, he was handsome. She could concede that much.

Oh, hell, who was she kidding? Michael wasn't merely handsome—he was the most striking man she'd ever met. He was dynamic and intelligent. He was the kind of man who made a woman drool. She'd been shocked and elated when he'd revealed his attraction to her. And the kiss they had shared made her want to curl her toes into the soles of her shoes.

But that's what made him so dangerous. He was the kind of man that tempted a woman to do things she normally wouldn't. Like lose sight of her hard-fought goals.

She wasn't going to let that happen. No, sir, she wasn't.

Chapter Eight

Michael inhaled the delicious aromas emanating from the take-out bags he carried from the car. Good food, wine, candles, flowers. The only element lacking for a romantic dinner was good company. And his was awaiting him in his condo.

He punched the elevator button and grinned, even though he was all alone. Sophia wasn't going to know what hit her. He had painstakingly planned an evening meant to both bewitch and bewilder her.

Silently slipping through the front door, he glanced at his watch. Perfect timing. According to the schedule he'd set for Hailey, Sophia should be giving his daughter a bath and getting her ready for bed. Seeing that the living room was empty, he hurried into the kitchen to make the necessary preparations. He could hear water running in the hallway bath and the sound of Sophia's soft crooning to Hailey made him smile.

His mother had been right. Sophia was great with Hailey. And Hailey seemed captivated by her nanny. However, the important motivating factor, as he saw it, was his awesome attraction to Sophia.

With the boxes of Chinese food warming in the oven, he turned his attention to setting the table.

He wanted a chance to explore the magnetism that drew him each and every time they were in a room together. Hell, they didn't have to be together for her—or rather thoughts of her—to pluck and pull at his attention.

It wasn't as if he were asking for promises of undying devotion. He merely wanted—*needed*—to delve into the allure that had taken hold of him.

He couldn't seem to quell the "ticking clock" feeling that had his gut all knotted up. Soon Sophia would find a suitable nanny to take her place. She'd told him she had her assistant working on doing just that. He realized it wasn't as if Sophia would be leaving town or anything, but once a replacement was found, she wouldn't be at his condo when he arrived home from work, and for some odd reason, he really liked the thought of her being there—in his apartment, taking care of his daughter—while he was busy at his office.

Michael decided to follow his mom's advice. He was going to attempt to woo Sophia before it was too late.

Warm candlelight gleamed against the shiny black ceramic plates and crystal goblets. He uncorked the wine and set it on the counter to breathe.

Once he'd taken the time to think about it, he realized his approach had been a little too straightforward, too in-your-face. He'd confronted Sophia. And what woman liked to be put on the spot like that? Anyone would have responded to that kind of blunt candor, especially when it was unexpected, with a negative reaction. Just as Sophia had done.

It seemed a little magic was in order. A little romance was called for. He had to sweep Sophia off her feet. Dazzle her with some soft music and delicious food, expensive wine and soft candlelight. He'd tried appealing to her logical mind, and he'd failed miserably. Now he needed to charm her senses.

He'd pondered and planned for days. And here it was Wednesday; he was ready.

A strategic phone call made this afternoon assured that Sophia would think he was working late, and that he needed her to feed Hailey, bathe her and tuck her into bed for the evening. Normally, that was his job—a job he'd come to love over these past weeks. The time he spent with Hailey each evening was special. Gazing into her tiny face, into those probing eyes, filled him with wonder as well as an amazing desire to protect. However, he had a unique assignment this evening. He would make up the time he missed with Hailey tomorrow.

He *had* worked an hour or so longer than usual, so he hadn't been lying to Sophia. But he'd left the office with a spring in his step and several stops to make before he could come home and execute his plan.

The light wood of the chopsticks contrasted nicely against the bold black color when he balanced them diagonally across the dinner plates.

"Hello? Michael?"

Sophia's query had him bolting to the kitchen doorway. He looked down the hall and lifted his hand in silent greeting. She'd wrapped Hailey in a soft terry towel and cradled his daughter to her chest. His heart swelled near to bursting.

"You're home. I thought—"

"I just arrived a few minutes ago. Got out of the office a bit earlier than I expected."

She nodded. "I smell food."

"I brought home dinner. I hope you're hungry."

"I'm starved. I had to eat my lunch on the run." She glanced down at the baby. "This one was a little pistol this afternoon. Skipped her nap and has been bright-eyed and bushy-tailed for hours. I wouldn't be surprised if she sleeps through the night."

While she spoke, Michael slowly advanced down the hallway. When he peeked at Hailey nestled in the yellow terrycloth, he saw that her damp hair was plastered to her head. He slid his index finger into her curled hand and she instinctively tightened her hold. She offered him a soft coo, velvety enough to bring the most hardened soul to his knees.

"Hey, there, princess," he whispered. "I missed you today."

He lifted his head, gazing into Sophia's cerulean eyes. *I missed you today, too,* he wanted to tell her, but didn't dare. There was time for all that. Later on tonight if he worked the proper magic.

A vibrant energy palpitated between them. Sophia nervously moistened her full lips.

Then Michael bent his head again and placed a gentle kiss on his little girl's cheek. He smelled baby scents mingling with the warm aroma of Sophia's skin. Need, steel-strong, coiled inside him. He turned his head the merest fraction and glimpsed Sophia's milky flesh where it met the collar of her blouse.

He straightened, his gaze sliding along the elegant length of her neck, along her jaw, over her delicate

130 NANNY AND THE BEAST

cheekbone. He wanted to press his nose to her temple, let his fingertips dance over her hair.

"Let me get her dressed and into bed," she told him, taking a short backward step. "I'll be right out."

Michael shrugged out of his suit jacket and tossed it across the living room chair on his way back into the kitchen. Excitement swirled in his belly. He clapped his hands and rubbed them together. He was a man on a mission. He would prove to Sophia without a shadow of a doubt that the attraction sparking between them was too bright, too intense to ignore. Rules, or no stinkin' rules.

He poured wine for them both, and then took the white boxes containing their dinner from the oven. The fancy control panel beeped at him when he pushed the off button. He considered transferring the food to fancy ceramic bowls, but decided that Chinese food was meant to be served directly from the distinctive white take-out cartons.

Opening each box, he inhaled the delicious aromas of dim sum and moo goo gai pan, stir-fried vegetables and Szechwan beef, and, of course, aromatic steamed jasmine rice that no Chinese meal would be complete without.

"My, my, just how hungry *are* you?"

Michael turned toward the kitchen doorway, the humor lacing Sophia's question making him smile. But it was her beautiful face that made his smile widen.

"I was just thinking I might have gone a bit over-board," he told her.

"I'll say." She moved to the table. "Everything smells wonderful, though. Thanks for the feast."

He pulled out a chair for her, and as she was settling

into it, he said, "You're very welcome. Thank you for taking such good care of Hailey today. I'm sorry I had to work late."

She caught his eye as he sat down. "When I first came to work for you, this was your normal arrival time."

He nodded. "It was, wasn't it? Seems that little girl's done something to me." He shook out a linen napkin and tucked it into his lap.

"She certainly has," Sophia commented. "You smile more now, too. And that's nice."

Hailey had a lot to do with the change in him, he was certain. But Sophia was a motivating factor, as well. He couldn't deny it.

"Fatherhood looks good on you."

The gratitude filling Michael's chest brightened his expression. Softly, he said, "You looked quite motherly yourself when I saw you with Hailey in the hallway a few minutes ago."

Oh. That remark had been a mistake. He'd obviously gotten too intimate too quickly. Sophia averted her gaze, looking uncomfortable.

He slid the container of dim sum toward her. "Let's eat."

His stumbling attempt to recover worked, it seemed. She reached for the appetizers, and after looking around for a serving spoon, she picked up her chopsticks. Then she glanced at him, the helplessness she felt expressed so clearly that he chuckled.

"Here," he offered, picking up his own, "let me show you how this works." He positioned the sticks properly and demonstrated how to maneuver them together to capture food. "It's easy, really. Give it a try."

She correctly rested one stick in the *v* between her

thumb and index finger, but then she curled her middle finger around it.

"No, no." He got up and went around behind her chair. "Hold them toward the end, not the middle," he instructed, bending over closer. "Like this." He let the bottom stick rest against the inside of the first knuckle of her ring finger. "Now hold the other one on top with your index and middle fingers. See?"

Sliding his hand around hers, he helped her to open and close the chopsticks. Although he couldn't see her face, he knew she was smiling. Being this close to her made his heart kick against his ribs with the strength of a young stallion.

Her hair smelled like sunshine, and her skin had a delicate aroma that made his mouth go dry.

"I think I've got it," she said, clearly delighted.

She turned her head just a small fraction, and her cheek brushed his. She went still. So did the atmosphere in the room.

Slow, man, he told himself sternly. *Go slow*.

He straightened and went back to sit at the table. He inched his chair in. "Use the chopsticks to move food onto your plate." She struggled to slide a small steamed dumpling. It took her several attempts, but she grinned when she succeeded.

He helped himself, saying, "If we were in China, we wouldn't have our own plates. The food would be placed on the table and everyone would just share."

"Really?" Her tone expressed true interest. She watched him lift a spring roll to his mouth and take a bite. "You're an expert with those things."

"Nowhere near it," he scoffed. "I'm lucky, though. I had some great teachers. Several clients who are originally from China. They were very patient with me." He finished off the spring roll, chewed and swallowed. "The first time we went out to dinner, I stuck my chopsticks into my rice. Everyone stopped eating and looked at me in horror."

"Uh-oh. Sounds like you made a faux pas."

"Oh, yes." He nodded. "I immediately retrieved the sticks from the rice and apologized. I quickly asked them to forgive my ignorance. They chuckled politely, and then I was told that I should never stick my chopsticks straight up in the rice bowl. Apparently, when someone passes away, the shrine contains a bowl of rice with two sticks of incense standing in it. My sticking my chopsticks into my rice was the equivalent to wishing death to someone at the table."

Sophia's lips parted in a small gasp and Michael laughed.

"Exactly," he said. "I was mortified."

He deftly helped himself to more of the appetizers.

"Your clients must have forgiven you," Sophia pointed out, "because you obviously had dinner with them again. And again. How else could you whip those sticks around like a ninja warrior at an all-you-can-eat buffet?" She looked at the chopsticks she held stiffly in her hand. "I'm afraid I'm going to starve to death."

Michael laughed. "You'll get the hang of it." But she looked so doubtful, he asked, "Do you want a fork?"

"Oh, no. How will I ever master this if I don't practice?"

"That's the spirit." Somehow, he had known that, if she hadn't already mastered the art of using chopsticks, she'd be willing to give it a try. Her enthusiastic nature was one of the things he liked about her.

They laughed through much of the meal, and he

wasn't surprised when he finished eating long before she did. However, she ate every bite in the traditional Asian manner—with her chopsticks—and she was quite pleased with herself when she was through.

She brought up the subject of Saturday's party. "Is there any last-minute shopping you'd like for me to do for you? Do you offer your employees gifts or anything?"

"I give them something they really appreciate. Money." He wiped his fingers on the napkin. "I hand out bonuses based on earnings records, and there's heavy competition to see who wins the top prize. Thanks for offering, but there's no need for shopping. I write out checks, and I'll have those ready beforehand."

"What are your plans for Hailey?" she asked. "I know you want to give people the chance to meet her, but…"

"I was thinking that I'd bathe her a little early." That probably sounded funny to Sophia coming from a stick-ler-for-the-rules such as himself. And he had pondered long and hard before deciding to veer off schedule, but Sophia had told him over and over his rules were too strict. Little by little, he was finding out how right she'd been. "Let everyone ooh and aah over my princess for a while, and then I'll put her to bed."

A pained expression pinched Sophia's eyebrows together.

"What?" he said.

"What if she doesn't cooperate? You know that—"

"Yes, yes. Babies are unpredictable." He chuckled. "And I don't mind saying that you are so right about that."

"It won't be much fun for you if she gets cranky."

"True."

"It will be difficult, if not impossible to play host and daddy at the same time."

"Also true." He picked up the bottle of wine and refilled their glasses.

"Would you like for me to work that night?"

"I can't have you working another weekend."

"Don't be silly. It's one evening. I could hide out in the nursery. No one would have to know I was here. If Hailey is cranky or refuses to go to sleep, I could entertain her so you can spend time with your guests."

"That would be great, Sophia. Thanks." He would rather she attend the party as his date, but he didn't dare push his luck.

"If she falls asleep right away," she said, "I could just slip out the door."

"That wouldn't be necessary." Trying to sound as if he'd just thought of the idea, he added, "You could join the party."

"Oh, I don't think that would be wise. This is a work thing. For both of us."

Refusing to let disappointment get him down, he stood. "Let's just play it by ear. I'm going to put these leftovers in the fridge."

"I'll help."

While they closed up the boxes and cleared the table, they talked about his parents' visit. As he closed the dishwasher door, he said, "My Dad enjoyed having dinner with you. Mom thought you were great."

"Your parents are wonderful people. You told me you have fond memories of your childhood, and with parents like those, I can see why."

Michael went to the table and picked up their glasses. "Let's take our wine into the living room." He handed her glass to her. "And you can tell me about *your* childhood."

She turned her back to him on her way into the living

room. "Oh, there's not a lot to tell. It certainly was no bed of roses."

Was that a tightness he detected in her tone?

"Don't get me wrong." Sophia rounded the coffee table and sat down on the sofa. "My brother and I weren't abused or anything. But our lives were…difficult."

He followed her and sat down on the couch next to her. "It was just the two of you?"

She nodded, smiling. "Me and Joe. He's my little brother." She chuckled. "It drives him nuts when I call him that. He's a teacher at a junior high in Dover. We're very close. Always have been." Her voice went soft as she added, "We had to be, really."

Michael hoped she would elaborate, but when she didn't, he probed further. "I guess he looked up to you?"

"He did. Just so long as he didn't feel I was being too strict with him."

Too strict with him? That was an odd choice of words for a sister to use about her brother.

"We went everywhere together."

Michael rested the base of his stemmed glass on his thigh. "So you took your job as big sister very seriously."

"Oh, yes. There was no reckless behavior in *my* past, I'll tell you that much. Joe really looked up to me, and besides that, he was all eyes and ears. The kid mimicked my every…" Her words trailed and alarm made her eyes widen the merest fraction. "Michael, I'm sorry. I didn't mean anything…with that stupid comment about being reckless. I wasn't meaning to bring up anything you might have—"

He waved his hand. "No offense taken. It's all right." One corner of his mouth curled. "I've taken full responsibility for my short spell of foolishness."

"You have," she quickly agreed.

After a brief pause, he said, "I do understand about a younger sibling wanting to act like an older brother or sister."

She looked surprised. "But I thought you were an only child?"

"I was. But I had a friend back in high school who was a couple of years older than I was, and we were close as brothers."

She lifted her wineglass to her lips.

"Dirk Simmons." Michael shook his head, memories flooding through his mind. "What a name, huh? Dirk. Sounds like a superhero or an arch-villain." He chuckled. "And he could be either-or, depending on his mood."

"Arch-villain." Sophia whistled softly. "I'll bet your mother was pleased to have her son looking up to such a character."

"Oh, Dirk didn't reveal his rebel side anywhere near my mother. He enjoyed her Sunday pot roast too much." Michael shifted on the couch, resting his arm along the back. "He wore his hair long. And he had the coolest black leather jacket. The girls flocked around him like he was some kind of rock star. Man—" he shook his head "—I thought he was something else. He told off a teacher once and was suspended for three days."

Sophia grinned. "And you looked up to this bad boy? I'm surprised at you, Michael."

"The girls loved him, though. Dirk didn't care what people thought of him."

"He cared what your mother thought," she reminded him.

"Well, yes. I guess I should say he didn't care what *most* people thought. He did what he wanted when he wanted."

Michael glanced to the far corner of the room, his tone going soft with contemplation. "The girls couldn't get enough of that devil-may-care manner of his."

"So you said…several times."

The humor lacing her words drew him back to the present. Laughing, he said, "I did, didn't I?" He sighed. "I wanted to be just like Dirk. But Dad took me to get a mandatory haircut every month, and Mom bought me nothing but polos and chinos and leather loafers."

Amusement glittered in Sophia's blue eyes. "It's hard to be a rebel in chinos and loafers."

"Tell me about it."

The whisper of a smile played on his mouth as he thought about his high school friend. Dirk had been slick and bold and dangerously reckless. All the guys had looked up to him, had wanted to *be* him.

"It couldn't have been all *that* bad."

"Hmm?" Michael asked, blinking.

"Being forced into the wholesome role, I mean," she said. "There were lots of clean-cut, respectable heroes to look up to. John Wayne, Willie Mays, Neil Armstrong." The corners of her eyes crinkled as she added, "And don't forget our favorite Jedi, Luke Skywalker."

They laughed, and Michael realized he'd never met a woman more delightfully surprising than Sophia. He felt a peculiar warmth somewhere in the vicinity of the middle of his chest.

"So…it was all good ol'—no, no—*bad* ol' Dirk's fault?" she teased.

Confusion slowly killed his grin. Evidently, she saw that he didn't understand.

"Your short spin around bad-boy land," she elaborated. "It was because of your admiration for your friend

Dirk that you tried out the rebel life once your success opened the door."

Michael went very still. "I never thought about it. But I guess you could be right. I was in awe of him, that's for sure." A sense of wonder overwhelmed him. "Could I have resented my own teen years that much? I was studious and straightlaced." He shook his head. "Wow. Could I have been subconsciously waiting to become another Dirk? To slip into that brash attitude? Rush into that reckless lifestyle?"

He didn't like the dark condemnation that cloaked him like a storm cloud.

"Hey, don't be so hard on yourself." Sophia reached out and touched his forearm. "You always wondered what it would be like to live with a brash attitude like Dirk's. And now you know. If you hadn't tried it, you'd have wondered the rest of your days."

She had a point, he realized. "And I did find out, really quickly, that the unrestrained life isn't for me. I discovered that my behavior *does* matter. That I *do* care what people think of me—my friends, my employees, my clients, my family."

The warmth that had hitched in his chest just moments before now oozed through his whole body. "I care what you think of me, Sophia."

He reached out and gently took the wineglass from her hand, and then he set both of them on the coffee table. Turning back to her, he reached up and cradled her gorgeous face between his hands.

An unfathomable expression hazed her eyes, and she went utterly motionless. He leaned forward and placed a soft kiss on her mouth. Her soft lips puckered just a bit as she kissed him back. Then her eyelids fluttered closed, her thick lashes tickling his cheek, and she sighed. Her breath brushed across his skin like warm silk.

"So whatever happened to him?" she whispered, her eyes still closed, her face a scant inch from his.

The question surprised Michael and he pulled back, sliding his hands from her jaw, down the curve of her neck, and resting them on her shoulders.

"What?" He felt discombobulated.

She opened her eyes, and desire darkened them to a vivid royal blue. Knowing that he had stirred such passion in her filled him with elation.

"Dirk. What happened to him?"

"Oh. Dirk." Michael inhaled a breath of mind-clearing air. "He's a pathologist. He lives in Chicago with his wife and their four daughters."

"A *pathologist*? You mean rebel Dirk is a science nerd?"

"Yeah, he is."

They both tried to contain their mirth, but all too quickly, it got the better of them.

She was in trouble. Deep trouble.

Sophia set the bottle of warm formula on a nearby table. She lifted Hailey to her shoulder and began patting the infant on her back with a firm, but gentle, touch.

Last night, Michael had surprised her when he'd brought dinner home with him. Even before dinner, though, some kind of kinetic energy had charged the atmosphere around them. She'd felt it when he'd come down the hall to greet his daughter after her bath. The birr stirring the air seemed to rush at her, full force, as he'd approached, and it had only become stronger the longer he'd stood near her.

The vital liveliness had swarmed them when she'd joined him in the kitchen where he'd set the table in a casual, but elegant, arrangement, complete with candles and flowers…and chopsticks.

She smiled even now, remembering how he'd chuckled at her first bumbling attempts to feed herself with the wooden utensils. He'd offered her a fork, but she'd wanted to be a good sport about it. Besides, she enjoyed trying new things and hadn't minded looking silly until she got the hang of maneuvering the chopsticks. Although she certainly hadn't become anything near adept, she had successfully finished her dinner with them.

Their conversation had been pleasant; Sophia found that, after caring for Hailey alone all day, she was starved for some adult interaction in the evenings.

And Michael had certainly given her more interaction than she'd bargained for last night.

As he'd told her more about his past—confided his intimate musing regarding the whys of his "bad boy" behavior—she'd become enthralled. He was a private man, and the fact that he opened himself up to her to such a degree had overwhelmed her.

When he'd taken her glass from her and caressed her face, his dark gaze had mesmerized her. Then he'd leaned toward her. Even now her heart pattered a staccato beat. Yes, their mouths had met for a fleeting moment, but that kiss had been so excruciatingly sweet, so romantic, that Sophia feared her heart was going to melt and trickle right down her rib cage.

The intimacy and sensuousness of the moment had lulled her to the point that she'd forgotten all about her decision to steer clear of romantic entanglements. She'd completely ignored her need for independence, her

choice of career over love, and she'd helplessly surren-
dered to Michael's tiny, but nonetheless steamy, kiss.

The man was a danger to everything she'd worked for.

Noticing that Hailey had fallen off to sleep, Sophia
placed the baby in the crib and covered her with a light
blanket. Knowing Hailey and her sleeping patterns well
by this point, Sophia realized she had about an hour and
forty minutes to make a few calls and—

The chirping of her cell phone had her reaching into
her pocket.

She flipped open the phone. "Sophia Stanton."

"Morning," Karen greeted. "How are you?"

"I was just going to call you. I'm well, thanks. Yourself?"

"I'm great." Her assistant's voice simmered with excitement. "I've got two new clients coming in for
consults today. One this morning and one this afternoon. Both have told me they're desperate for childcare.
I think I'll have two nannies well on their way to being
placed before the workday is over."

"That's wonderful, Karen. I know I've told you this
several times over the past couple of weeks, but I have
to say it again. You're doing an excellent job there."

"Thanks, Sophia. I'm really enjoying working full-
time." She laughed. "I like the extra money, too."

"I'm sure you do." Karen's mention of her wage
increase started Sophia thinking. She walked out of the
nursery, pulling the door closed behind her. "Karen, I
want you to call Fay Richardson today. Ask her if she'll
consider coming to work for Mr. Taylor if he were to
offer her a pay raise."

"But what will the Harrisons do for a nanny?"
Karen asked.

"You'll give them a new one."

"But you've never shuffled nannies before."

"I'm desperate," Sophia said. "I told Michael I'd find him someone suitable. Fay is everything he's looking for."

"But—"

"No more buts, Karen. Just call Fay."

Karen went quiet. "What's wrong, Sophia?"

Her mouth went flat. Then she said, "Things here have become…awkward."

"Is that man bullying you?"

Sophia almost smiled. "No, Karen. He's not bullying me. But our relationship is becoming…uncomfortable for me."

"Fay won't like working for someone who's difficult."

"He's not difficult." She failed to quell the sharpness in her tone.

"Sophia, what's going on there?"

"Nothing, Karen. Nothing. Okay?" However, she knew the swiftness of her response said otherwise.

"Oh, I think it's something." Karen inhaled a breathy gasp. "You two are making it, aren't you?"

"We are doing no such thing." Sophia wondered how the conversation had gotten so out of hand.

"Well, you're doing *something*. I can tell." With mirth in her tone, Karen concluded, "And if he's not treating you bad, then he must be treating you good."

Frustration had Sophia blurting, "He kissed me, okay? But it didn't mean anything."

She refused to mention that they'd kissed twice, and that she was desperate to find someone to take her place because she feared that the growing intimacy might soon begin to mean *some*thing.

Hell, who was she kidding? It already meant something. What, exactly, she was too afraid to determine. But she could feel it deep in her bones. The man was getting to her. She needed to find a nanny for Hailey so she could put some space between herself and Michael.

"I'll call Fay," Karen promised quietly.

"Thanks." Sophia heaved a sigh of relief. "Call me the minute you know something."

She heard what she thought was a muffled giggle.

"You kissing Mr. Taylor kinda brings new meaning to our company motto, don't you think?" Karen teased. "No client left unsatisfied."

Sophia gritted her teeth and disconnected the call.

Chapter Nine

"**I**'m in trouble. Deep trouble."

Flicker, Sophia's neglected tabby, was purring so loudly in her lap that she could barely hear Michael's words over the phone, but the distress in his tone had her sitting up straighter. It was Saturday morning, and she'd just left Michael and Hailey an hour and a half ago. She'd arrived home, tossed a load of clothes into the washer, cleaned out the litter box, sorted the mail, filled out a few bills and she'd been giving Flicker some much needed attention while contemplating her remaining chores and errands when the phone had rung.

When she'd left him, things had been copacetic. He'd seemed pleased to discover that a granny-type nanny would arrive on Monday, and all plans for his employee appreciation party scheduled for this evening were falling into place. Sophia would arrive to man the nursery, but she didn't think she'd be staying very long.

Hailey would most probably sleep until her one o'clock feeding, which Michael would be responsible for.

That alluring current continued to drone between herself and Michael, and she'd been relieved to get a break from the tension with a few hours away from him. She hadn't expected to hear from him so soon.

"What is it, Michael?" she asked, sliding Flicker off her lap and onto the couch cushion. "Is Hailey ill?"

"No, she's fine. But the caterer called." The tension he was feeling snapped and sparked over the phone line. "Apparently, the new office manager overbooked the staff. They don't have enough employees to supply all the jobs they have for this evening. The food isn't a problem, but they can't send anyone to serve."

"Well, that shouldn't be too much of a prob—"

"Sophia," he barked, "I was supposed to have someone manning the kitchen, two people serving and one tending bar. Where am I going to find four warm bodies to help me? This gathering was supposed to be honoring the people who work for me. I'd rather cancel the whole thing than ask them to work during the party. That's not what I had in mind at all—"

"You've got me," she reminded him. "I'll be there."

"But I need you to help me with Hailey."

It sounded as if his blood pressure was on the rise.

"Calm down, Michael. Let me think." Flicker refused to leave her alone, so she nudged the cat away, stood and paced across the room. "This is a paying gig, right?"

"I'll pay top dollar. Why? Do you know anyone who might be willing to help on such short notice?"

Mirth, tactless at a time like this, but fitting as well, had her pressing her lips together. "Remember those nannies you fired? One of them worked as a bartender before earning her childcare certification. And I know Lily is working for a family that gives her weekends off. My assistant might be free, as well." Her mind whirred. "Let me make some calls, and I'll get right back to you."

"Someone to mix drinks would be great, Sophia." He sounded much more at ease. "And a couple people to serve the food would be—"

"I can't promise anything." She hated to burst his bubble, but she had to be honest. "Cheryl—the young woman with bartending experience—was scared witless of you after you fired her. She might not agree to work for you again."

Michael sighed. "I guess I was rough on the girls who first came to take care of Hailey. But I was…well, I thought I should…I wasn't sure…" Again, he sighed. "I didn't know what I was doing, Sophia. Hailey frightened me to death. She was tiny. Perfectly helpless. And what the heck did I know about babies? It feels like all that happened years ago rather than weeks. All I knew then was that I wanted to be the best damn father I could be. I wanted to give Hailey the best I could…so I came up with a plan that I thought would make that possible. It never occurred to me that the rules I'd come up with might be too…harsh. For a baby, I mean."

It was a heartfelt confession. And although Sophia was relieved to hear that she'd figured out his motives before he had, she was even more relieved that he'd figured it out for himself.

"I know, Michael," she told him softly. "You only had the best of intentions. I understand that. I'm glad you understand that, too."

"If not for you, I don't think I'd have come to understand them at all."

Sophia remained silent.

"Because you were willing to explain things to me," he continued—

What she'd been willing to do, Sophia thought, was *confront* him about the error in his thinking about Hailey. The other nannies who had worked for him had been too timid to do that.

"—I was able to finally work out the truth. About my rules. And about my daughter's needs. Thank you, Sophia."

His tone softened and intensified when he uttered her name, and a shiver coursed through her. Sophia pressed her splayed palm to her diaphragm in an attempt to soothe the twitter burbling there. Those honeyed words could easily make her drunk; listening to them was risky.

"Y-you're welcome." Awkwardness tied her tongue in knots. She suddenly felt frantic to change the topic and the tone of this conversation. "Michael, if I'm going to rustle up some help for tonight, I'd better start making those calls."

"Of course. I can't express my appreciation for all you've done for me."

"Oh," she said, "before I forget. If the girls are able to come, they'll want to know what they should wear."

"No dress code tonight. This is a celebration. Tell them to put on their party dresses."

Michael stood in a far corner of the living room attempting to focus on a conversation taking place between several of his employees; however, once again, he found himself gazing across the room at the woman who was holding his baby girl.

Could that really be the nanny who'd been living in his home for the past several weeks?

The change in Sophia was as astounding as it was breathtaking. The figure-hugging dress she wore was the color of fine claret, a hue that accentuated her smooth skin and played up the rich and shiny golden red tones in her wavy chestnut hair. The neckline wasn't unseemly low, but it did reveal a bit of cleavage, and the hemline, although just an inch or two above her knees, exposed shapely legs. She'd obviously used the normal female paraphernalia to emphasize her blue eyes, her high cheekbones and her lush, glistening mouth.

It wasn't as if he hadn't realized she was a beautiful woman before tonight. Her cerulean eyes flashed with both an appeal and intelligence that had captured his attention right away. And he'd already kissed her twice, so he knew those lips were honey sweet. He'd seen her in casual clothing—jeans and top—when they'd had dinner with his parents, and she'd even worn a bit of gloss and glamour that night, too.

But tonight she was beautiful.

He'd specified that the nannies who worked for him were to dress discreetly, tie back their hair and wear minimal, if any, makeup. His goal had been to prompt the women to focus solely on the care of his daughter. But now he was left wondering what he'd missed. Sophia was nothing short of stunning.

As the party unfolded, a few of his male employees had made some less-than-subtle inquiries about her— Tyrell had come right out with a low, appreciative whistle before commenting that the woman didn't look like any nanny he'd ever seen—and Michael's mood had turned dark.

Sophia had become a veritable lifesaver for him. She'd salvaged the evening, of that he was certain. Had she not come through with some of her nannies to help him pull off this party, he'd have been up the creek without a paddle. There would have been no other option for him but to cancel.

"She's something else."

Anthony's comment snapped Michael back to the here and now. He glanced at the man, and quickly noticed that the small group he'd been talking with had drifted away.

"Do you mind if I ask her for her number?" Anthony asked, not taking his eyes off Sophia.

"Actually, I do." The gruffness abrading his tone surprised him. Anthony was one of his top earners. There was a fat bonus check with his name on it enclosed in one of the many envelopes Michael intended to give out a little later. Anthony would have to be satisfied with a money prize tonight because he certainly wasn't going to walk away with Sophia's number. Not if Michael had any say in the matter, anyway.

Anthony lifted his hands up in quick surrender. "Hey, sorry. I didn't know you had designs on the lady. Forget I said anything." After offering his boss an amiable smile, Anthony moved on to join another group.

Although Sophia had drawn him from the very first, Michael hadn't been interested in exploring the attraction initially. He'd just been burned. Badly. And he'd been more intent on figuring out how and why Ray Anne had been able to dupe him so completely and thoroughly. Over the course of a couple of weeks, he'd been able to work it all out, though…all because Sophia had made him think. She'd challenged his beliefs in a lot of things, actually.

It had been easy to figure out that Sophia was nothing like Ray Anne, and that the chemistry between them was strong.

Oh, yes, he had designs on the woman. Yes, he did.

When she had told him she'd found the perfect nanny for Hailey, an older, more experienced woman named Fay Richardson who met all his requirements, Michael had experienced vastly conflicting feelings. He'd been relieved that his daughter would have the best care available and happy that Sophia had come through for him, but he was also sad that she would no longer be available on a day-to-day basis. However, he'd been mollified by the notion that he knew where she worked, where she lived; he knew how to contact her. Having a new nanny in his home wouldn't be the end of the world. And having a new nanny didn't mean he couldn't continue following his mother's advice. He could carry on wooing Sophia. He'd just have to be more creative in his tactics.

Three short weeks was probably not enough time to start tossing around the big *L* word. But Michael was fairly certain that Sophia had stolen his heart. All he had to do now was make her realize the depth of his emotions.

He found himself searching the room, and when his eyes met hers, she motioned him to her. He made his way through the mass of people to the other side of the room.

"She's getting fussy," Sophia told Michael, patting Hailey in an attempt to soothe her. "It's way past her bedtime. Do you mind if I take her to the nursery? I think everyone's had a chance to meet her."

Many of the people who came tonight had brought Hailey a little something; a stuffed animal or a toy that rattled or lit up. His baby girl had been the center of attention for quite a while, especially with his female employees.

"I'll feed her, change her and then tuck her into bed," Sophia continued.

"I think that would be a good idea." Michael took Hailey into his arms and nuzzled her warm neck with his nose. He loved the delicate, clean scent of her. Hailey gazed intently at him with her dark eyes for a moment and love knotted in his throat. His little girl had a way of reminding him of what a miracle life could be. He kissed both of her soft cheeks before handing her back to Sophia.

"You'll hang around, won't you?" he asked Sophia quietly. "After you get Hailey to sleep?"

She nodded. "Karen's going to need my help in the kitchen. Cheryl's been so busy at the bar that Karen's had to hustle to keep the buffet stocked."

Sophia had had a difficult time finding adequate help for Michael's party. Lily and Isabel both had plans and had told Sophia they wouldn't work for the man who had fired them even if they'd been free. After numerous phone calls that left her feeling as if she were close to failure, Sophia finally talked Karen into rescheduling dinner with her parents as a special favor to her. Cheryl, the young woman with bartending experience, had been available but exceedingly reluctant to tangle with The Beast again, having left his home in tears just a month or so ago and acquiring the title of being the first nanny he'd fired. Sophia assured Cheryl that Michael had become much more amenable these days and that he would be truly grateful to have her help.

Sophia lifted Hailey to her shoulder. "I'm sorry I wasn't able to find more help."

He touched her then, sliding his fingers over her

upper arm and giving her a gentle squeeze. Sophia felt jolted by the heat of him.

"Don't apologize," he said, his voice whispery soft. "I can't thank you enough for all you've done to help me make this evening a success."

Appreciation curled his mouth into a smile, but then the muscles of his face relaxed, his smile waned and something intense illuminated his deep brown eyes.

"Hey, boss," Tyrell called from several yards away, "isn't it time for the speeches?"

Michael glanced away from her then, but she couldn't seem to tear her gaze away from his profile. He had a firm jaw, and she liked the play of muscle just beneath his swarthy, clean-shaven skin when he smiled at the people in the room. His cologne had her wanting to lean closer to him. The distinct sense of authority seemed to emanate from him and Sophia found it too appealing.

She let her eyelids flutter closed, fearful that her feelings for Michael were growing way out of safe proportion and thankful that Fay would be arriving early Monday morning to begin her stint as Hailey's nanny. She'd been uncomfortable all night long at the longing glances Michael had been casting her way. This attraction between the two of them was getting out of hand.

All she had to do, she kept promising herself silently, was get through the evening. After that, her obligation to him would be met and she could get back to normal life as she knew it.

"I'll be right there," he said to his guests. Michael directed his attention to Sophia once again. "I'm going to ask Karen and Cheryl to take a break in the kitchen while I give out the bonuses. They can rest a while and get a little something to eat."

She nodded and then headed off to the kitchen. With Karen hovering around the buffet in the dining room, the kitchen was empty as Sophia heated the bottle of formula.

In the nursery, Sophia took her time feeding Hailey. This sweet infant had come to mean just as much to Sophia as her daddy had. It was going to be difficult to go into the office on Monday, rather than coming here and caring for this precious bundle of joy. Hailey and Sophia had truly bonded over these past weeks. So many times, Sophia had found herself dreaming of babies and white picket fences while rocking Hailey to sleep. However, she'd tried hard to keep her mind wrapped around the cold, hard fact that this was a temporary arrangement made to save her business reputation.

Sophia feared that Hailey would suffer a touch of separation anxiety. She was certain *she* would experience some angst next week at the office. Of course, she'd survive, she'd eventually get used to missing Hailey—and Fay was so good with children that Sophia was confident that the elderly woman would do a great job of smoothing this new transition for the baby.

The pretty pink quilt tucked around Hailey's shoulders would keep her warm through the night. Sophia rested her hands on the crib railing and stared for another few moments, her heart constricting almost painfully as she tamped down a jumble of conflicting emotions. A lump rose in her throat when she left the nursery and quietly closed the door behind her.

Michael was still talking to his guest when Sophia slipped into the kitchen. Karen and Cheryl were sitting at the table, both enjoying an array of gourmet fare from the buffet table.

"The crab balls are wonderful, Sophia," Cheryl said. "You ought to try some. And the grilled scallops are to die for. But be careful, the cocktail sauce is a little on the spicy side."

"Yeah," Karen agreed, heavy mischief tugging at her features, "but that's not the only spiciness being served up this evening."

Sophia picked up a glass from the counter and filled it with water, eyeing her assistant all the while. "What are you going on about?" she asked lightly.

"Oh, I think you're well aware of the fiery looks that have been shooting your way by the host of the evening. It's as if The Beast is on the hunt and you're his prey." Karen grinned as she dipped a small spring roll into sweet-and-sour sauce and popped it into her mouth.

Great, Sophia thought. Just what she needed. The first sparks of a white-hot "office gossip" bonfire that would have everyone connected with The Nanny Place buzzing for days on end.

"Karen, you're a professional," she admonished. "You know better than to natter on like that about a client, especially in his own home."

Her assistant flapped her hand in the air. "Oh, he can't hear me. He's busy with his party guests. Listen to that laughter in there."

Before Sophia could expound on the reprimand, Cheryl said, "I saw it, too, Sophia. I don't understand how anyone can argue against the facts. Mr. Taylor's got the hots for you, that much is obvious. And from the looks he's been giving you all night, he's got it *bad.*"

"Now, look here, you two—"

"Look who's talking, Sophia," Karen said. "You're the one who started the name-calling. Cheryl, you weren't in the office the day Mr. Taylor marched in there firing nannies and shouting orders and making demands, not to mention threatening to cancel his contract." Karen eyes were wide. "Lily was there, though. She can vouch that what I'm saying is the utter truth. Once he'd stormed out and the dust had settled, the last thing this one did—" she indicated to Sophia with a sharp jab of her thumb "—before leaving the office that day was to make a solemn vow to tame The Beast."

Sophia crossed her arms over her chest, her face going tight with disapproval, but the two young women seemed bent on ignoring her.

Cheryl chuckled. "Ah, so it was all part of a diabolical plan. And I can see that you've succeeded famously. That man is good and tame, that's for sure. Judging from the misty-eyed stupor he's in, he's more than tame, actually."

"Yeah, Sophia," Karen teased unmercifully, "you could make him your love slave. Tell the truth. That's what you had in mind all along, wasn't it?"

Sophia rolled her eyes. "Do you two realize how immature you…" The rest of her scolding comment went unspoken when she realized their attention had been drawn to the kitchen doorway, their mirth dying faster than a water-doused flame.

A weighty lump formed in her gut. Before she turned, she knew whom she would find standing there. And all too quickly she discovered she was correct.

Acrid emotion set Michael's face into a staunch and steely mask as he stood in the kitchen doorway.

"We're ready for the champagne now," he said to anyone who happened to be listening, and then he was gone.

"Oh, no," Karen whispered. "Do you think he overheard us?"

His angry gaze had connected with Sophia's for only the briefest of moments before he'd disappeared from view, but it had been long enough for her to recognize without a doubt that he certainly had heard their conversation, or a good portion of it, anyway.

"I think the question we should be asking," Cheryl intoned, "is *how much* did he hear?"

"Enough." Sophia sighed heavily. "He heard enough."

"I'm afraid you're right." Karen snatched up her napkin and anxiously began wiping her fingers as she got up from the chair. "Did you see the look on his face?"

Cheryl's green eyes were hooded with worry when she, too, stood. "What should we do?"

"We should go in there and serve the champagne." Sophia let her arms fall loosely to her sides.

"But—"

"But—"

Both young women started off in seamless harmony.

"Didn't you see him?" Karen looked downright fearful.

"He's furious," Cheryl finished.

"Yes, I saw." Sophia shooed them toward the door. "And, yes, it's obvious that he's furious. But we've got a job to do. Let's go do it. I'll apologize to him later."

While the women busied themselves at the makeshift bar filling the crystal flute glasses with the sweet-scented champagne, Sophia took a moment to cast a quick glimpse around the room in search of Michael and caught his gaze, dark and disenchanted, on her. But the air chilled as if it had been frozen, and he turned away.

She hated the idea that he might be thinking she was an unscrupulous schemer who had come into his home with nefarious motives. But then she paused, the sudden halt causing a dribble of champagne to puddle on the top of the table. Maybe…just maybe, this could be for the best.

Chapter Ten

She couldn't do it, she finally decided. Leaving Michael's house with him thinking she'd been scamming him became less and less a possibility the longer she thought about it.

The party was winding down. Even now, Michael was saying goodbye to a group of his guests at the front door while Sophia made a final sweep of the living room in search of crumpled napkins, dirty glasses and forgotten hors d'oeuvre plates.

It had dawned on her that Michael had had his fill of conniving women after having been blackmailed by Hailey's mother. He'd confessed to feeling embarrassed by his own behavior, of having allowed himself to be tricked by the baby's mother. But he'd been hurt, too. It would have been impossible for him not to be wounded when he'd discovered that a woman he'd been dating was not who and what he'd thought her to be.

Oh, he'd have been angry, too. Just as he was now. A man as dynamic as Michael would have been furious at having been robbed of control like that, to have someone else calling the shots, not to mention blackmailing him for a fortune. But Sophia suspected that he used his anger to cover his more vulnerable emotions. Emotions he wasn't comfortable dealing with.

She couldn't stand the idea that she might cause him the same kind of upset and grief as Ray Anne had. There was no way on earth that Sophia wanted him to plunk her in the same category as that horrible, devious woman. She wouldn't be able to live with herself unless she attempted to explain.

Waltzing into the kitchen, she set the dishes on the counter by the sink and tossed the paper napkins into the trash. Cheryl's shoulders looked tight with tension as she stood at the sink, her hands in sudsy water nearly to the elbows. She kept glancing toward the doorway as if any second she expected to see a monster—or a beast—charge in for the attack. Karen stood next to Cheryl plucking stemware from the drainer and drying glasses as if her life depended on how quickly she finished the job.

"I think we should face him together," Karen said. "We'll say we're sorry, and then we'll get out quick. There's only one guy who's still here, and he's hanging around back in the office."

Cheryl's expression looked pained. "That's Mark, and he's hanging around waiting for me. We're going out for a beer."

"No way." Karen's frantic drying ceased. "You can't leave us to face Mr. Taylor alone. He's been glowering at us ever since—"

"It's okay," Sophia placated. "Both of you can go. I'll talk to Michael by myself."

"I can't let you do that," Karen said. "He'll chew you up."

Sophia smiled. "If I've learned anything while working for the man, it's that his bark is far worse than his bite. I'll be all right. Yes, it'll be uncomfortable, but I'll straighten everything out." She held up a towel for Cheryl. "There's not much left to be done here. A few glasses and plates to wash and put away. I'll finish up."

"You're sure?" Cheryl asked, eagerly accepting the towel and patting her hands dry.

The room seemed to contract when Michael entered the kitchen. He held three white envelopes in his hand.

"I calculated the total amount of what the catering service would have charged me for servers and I divvied it up equally among the three of you." He handed one envelope to each of them, then looked from Cheryl to Karen. "I'm pleased with your work. And I'm grateful that you showed up tonight to help." The crease knitting his forehead seemed to belie the statement. "You've worked hard. You can go on home. In fact, Mark is out there waiting for one of you, I believe." Then he nailed Sophia with a hard look. "I need you to stay for a few minutes."

It wasn't an invitation; it was a demand. It seemed The Beast had returned full-force and in need of being in complete control.

Cheryl peeked inside the envelope Michael had given her, her face yielding to cheery surprise. Sophia had known he would be generous.

Karen caught Sophia's eye, a silent question in her gaze. Sophia offered a tiny nod to let her friend know that she would be just fine.

"We'll see ourselves out," Cheryl said over her shoulder on her way out of the kitchen.

Anxiety continued to etch Karen's countenance. "Call me, Sophia."

"I will," she assured her easily. Determined not to let Michael bully her, she set her envelope on the counter, went to the sink and took up washing the dishes where Cheryl left off.

For several long, drawn-out minutes he was quiet, busying himself with tidying up the kitchen. The sound of the front door opening and closing filtered into the room, and an unnatural stillness fell over the condo. Finally, he picked up the towel, plucked a plate from the dish rack and began drying.

The warm mass of him so close to her felt oddly familiar, and would have been pleasant had the air in the room not been so strained.

"I never would have believed—" his voice was tight "—that you were the kind of person who would come up with a diabolical plan."

The fact that he'd used Cheryl's exact phrasing alerted Sophia to the fact that he'd been eavesdropping longer than she'd suspected.

"But it's clear that, once again, I have made a terrible misjudgment of character."

"You haven't misjudged me, Michael." Tiny white bubbles dripped from Sophia's hands when she pulled them from the dishwater. "But you are misconstruing the conversation you heard."

"Ah, I see." He continued to wipe the plate although it was already bone dry. "So you didn't dub me with a mean nickname?"

Heat flushed her face and she averted her gaze back

to the sudsy water when she was forced to admit, "I'm uncertain about who exactly came up with it."

"And you didn't vow to 'tame The Beast'?"

Terribly discomfited, Sophia sighed. Quietly, she said, "That sounds terrible taken out of context."

"Yes, it does." His tone was sharply honed. "So why don't you put it into context for me?" He set the plate down on the counter with a thump. "Set it up. Paint a picture. Help me to understand the situation, the motives that would have you calling me rude names and plotting against me."

She tried to hold onto the thought that he'd been deceived by a woman before. He'd been played for a fool once, and he was under the impression that he was being played for a fool all over again. He deserved a little leeway here. But her grasp on that notion was swiftly slipping in the shadow of his holier-than-thou attitude. How could he stand there and act as if he were utterly blameless in this mess?

Plunking her fists on her hips, she said, "I'll be happy to paint a picture for you, Michael." Damp spots spread under her hands, but she ignored them. "You burst into The Nanny Place demanding a nanny immediately. Immediately meaning, *that day*. Normally, it takes time to match a nanny to a family. Most importantly to the child. But would you allow me to utilize a technique that's proved successful many times over? No. You insisted on bucking the system. And I did everything I could to accommodate you."

She reached out and snatched a paper towel from the dispenser and swiped at her hands. "Then you started firing my nannies. And each and every one of them came back to the office reporting what an inflexible, bull-headed boss you were. Yes, we started calling you The Beast. Yes, it was wrong and I apologize." She chucked the crumpled paper towel into the trash can. "However, you know what they say about a shoe that fits."

Anger roiled through her, surprising her with its intensity. "And then you stormed into my office threatening to cancel your contract and promising to tell everyone you know that The Nanny Place had failed to satisfy your needs. I had no choice but to leave my business in the hands of my assistant, who up until that moment had only been a part-time employee. I was very unhappy that day, Michael. No, I was fuming. And worried sick about making a choice that very well might jeopardize my business." She lifted her hands, palm up. "It was in *that* context, in the heat of *that* moment, that I promised the girls in the office—hell, I promised myself—that I meant to tame The Beast. Yes, I said it. I used those very words."

She'd sent Cheryl and Karen home so she could calmly explain things, so he wouldn't think she was some kind of conniving miscreant like the woman who had tricked him. Yet here she was, wild-eyed, hand-waving and raging like an angry lunatic.

Her deep inhalation made her chest rise. She closed her eyes for a moment and moistened her lips. Her anger seemed to dissipate almost as quickly as it had been touched off.

"After I arrived," she continued, suddenly weary, "and realized that your overbearing behavior was your way of trying to compensate for your ignorance—"

Her choice of words took him aback and his reaction had her clamping her mouth shut.

She tried again. "I wasn't inferring that you're

ignorant. I meant your lack of knowledge. About babies. You didn't know what you were doing, so you came up with a bunch of rules and regulations to help you control things, that you felt would work."

He frowned. "You had all that figured out back then?"

"Yes," she admitted. "But, as we both discovered, most of your rules didn't work." Gently, she added, "Babies don't follow rules, Michael. You've said so yourself."

He looked visibly subdued, and Sophia couldn't tell if it had been her words or the fact that she'd let go of her annoyance and was using a softer tone.

Michael dropped the towel he'd been holding on to the dish he'd dried. He sighed as he raked his fingers through his hair.

"I have, Sophia."

They stood in the quiet, staring at each other.

Finally, she said, "Once I figured out why you were acting so…brutish about Hailey's care, I realized I could help you. That I could help Hailey, too. And I think I've done that. I'm sure you know I have." She flattened her mouth, wanting to smile but unsure if he was ready to make peace. "I'm sorry. I'm sorry we called you names. And I'm sorry that I—"

He raised his hand and shook his head. "No. I'm the one who should be sorry. I deserved it. Everything. I was mean and overbearing to the nannies you sent. I was hard on you, too. And I needed someone to put me in my place." He scrubbed at the back of his neck. "But I had the best of intentions."

"I know you did."

"And about tonight—" he paused, searching her face. "I shouldn't have unleashed my anger like I did. Even after what I heard. I know you. We've spent a lot of time together, Sophia. I should have realized there would be a reasonable explanation. I should have thought the best of you, not the worst of you." He frowned. "But it's difficult for me."

After what he'd been through, his Pavlovian response was quite normal, Sophia surmised. She nodded. "I know."

Obviously ill at ease, he shifted his weight from one foot to the other.

"So we're okay, you and I?" he asked.

His utter sincerity warmed her heart. "We're okay."

The tension in his shoulders eased and he smiled, and the heat inside her flared. Why did she react so physically to this man?

"This is it, then?" He tilted his head. "You're no longer Hailey's nanny?"

"You'll like Fay. I'm sure of it. She's exactly what you've wanted all along."

His head bobbed twice. "I'm sure you're right." His dark gaze leveled on hers. "I trust you."

That infamous, enigmatic flux began to eddy around her and she found it difficult to draw a breath. He looked like he had more to say.

She swallowed nervously and made a quarter turn toward the door. "It's really getting late. I should be going."

"Of course," he told her. "I'll get your wrap."

At the door, he thanked her again for her help with the party. Then he thanked her for her help with Hailey. Then he expressed his appreciation for her patience with him as he was learning what it meant to be a parent. The forth time he thanked her, Sophia let loose soft, uneasy laughter.

She slipped her shawl over her shoulders. "You're welcome. For everything."

But still he didn't say goodbye, and instinct told her he was stalling. He wanted the evening to linger.

"I have to go," she said. "Good night, Michael."

"Sophia." Something significant constricted his handsome features. "I'd like to see you."

"If you have any questions that Fay can't answer, or if you—"

"Wait." He frowned. "I didn't mean professionally. Let me rephrase that."

There was no need for him to restate anything. His aim had been perfectly clear to her. But she'd purposefully misinterpreted him, postponing the inevitable.

"Please don't." She gathered her shawl closer around her. "Michael, I've already explained that I can't get involved—"

"But that's just it. You haven't explained."

Why was he determined to make this difficult? It was simply the nature of the beast, she guessed. No pun intended. He was a man who wanted what he wanted… and usually got it. But he wasn't going to succeed this time around.

"I've made some important choices for my life, Michael. I'm on a set path. Blazing a course that I refuse to abandon. A course that doesn't include a man. A course that doesn't include you."

There. It was out. She couldn't have been clearer or more specific.

An inscrutable expression clouded his gaze. He was probably feeling hurt. Rejected. But she couldn't concern herself with that. He was a big boy. He'd get over it.

With nothing more to say, she walked out the door.

* * *

When a person worked in investments, he didn't dally with losing odds. If he saw his capital diminishing, if his assets showed signs of depreciation, he took action. Dwelling on any particular situation for too long only resulted in an ever-increasing risk of suffering a revenue thrashing. When the market showed signs of a down-turn, a good investor acted swiftly. Decisively. Whether on behalf of himself or a client; he cut his losses, and he moved on. Another business venture was always waiting in the wings.

However, Michael was realizing that when it came to personal matters, he often didn't use good sense. He'd moped around the house all day, and here it was Sunday night. He had work tomorrow. He had portfolios he should be studying, accounts and stocks and commodities he should be monitoring so he'd be ready to discuss them with his team first thing in the morning. Yet all he could think about was Sophia and that cryptic malarkey she'd prattled off before leaving last night.

Hailey sighed in his arms, and he gazed at her lovely face. He tucked the blanket around her more securely and continued to rock. She'd polished off her formula and had been sleeping for at least ten minutes, but he continued to hold her.

His daughter was a joy. The only bright spot in his life at the moment, it seemed. Several times over the course of the day, he'd become so involved with feeding her, or engaging her, or changing her, or bathing her, that he'd forgotten his worries, his heart had grown light, and he'd even found himself chuckling once or twice when Hailey caught and held his gaze. He'd read babies as young as his daughter weren't able to grin and that their facial expressions were involuntary reflexes, but he didn't believe that for a moment. For long moments, he and Hailey connected, and she would do her darnedest to express herself with smiles and frowns, sighs and tears.

Every day, he grew more confident in his paternal role. But he couldn't kid himself. This self-assurance was mainly due to the fact that Sophia had forced him to recognize how off-target he'd been about babies in general. She'd essentially taken him by the hand and trained him regarding Hailey's needs. Oh, he was certain that he'd have learned all that was necessary to be a good father. Eventually. But because Sophia hadn't been afraid to speak her mind, to tell him when he'd been wrong, she'd enabled him to gather much more understanding in a shorter time span.

Gently, he placed the baby in her crib on her side, just as Sophia had shown him. He lovingly smoothed the folds from the blanket and then closed the door of the nursery on his way out.

He went into the living room and saw the envelope containing Sophia's payment sitting on the coffee table, stark white against the smoky glass. In her haste to get out the door, she'd left it behind last night.

I've made some important choices for my life, Michael. I'm on a set path.

Her words echoed through his head.

Some important choices? What kind of vague nonsense was that?

Michael shoved the newspaper aside and plopped down onto the sofa.

What difference did it make what kind of nonsense it was? Sophia had plainly stated that she wasn't interested in him.

He swiped a hand across his mouth and chin. But she *was* interested. She was attracted to him. He'd seen it in her eyes, tasted it in her kiss. And she'd been just as aware as he was of that strong magnetic energy that tugged at them whenever they were within sight of one another.

So it wasn't that she wasn't interested. It was that she was making a conscious effort to avoid becoming intimately involved.

But why?

Frustration had him shoving his way off the sofa. He folded the newspaper into some semblance of order, and then he stalked toward the back of the condo to his office.

Answers. Where the hell could he find some answers? He wasn't going to put this to rest until he got some kind of logical explanation. And Sophia certainly wasn't going to offer him anything of the sort.

He sat down at his desk, moving the mouse so his computer would kick itself out of hibernation mode. Without even thinking about what he was doing, he clicked the link that took him to the national white pages. The phone book. Slowly, he punched the letters in the search box.

Joe Stanton.

Dover, DE.

Faster than he could blink, Joseph Stanton's home address and telephone number popped up onto the screen.

Michael scrubbed at his face. What was he thinking? Calling Sophia's brother was a crazy idea. What could he possibly say to the man that would move him to reveal personal information about his sister?

He tried several opening lines in his head, deciding that he sounded just shy of a total, raving lunatic. So he was astonished when he picked up the phone and began dialing anyway.

Although the man sounded approachable enough when he answered on the third ring, Michael's gut still twisted in a knot. The first thing he had to do was verify that he'd called the correct number.

After identifying himself, he asked, "Do you have a sister name Sophia who owns The Nanny Place?"

"I do." His voice went tight with alarm. "Is Sophia all right?"

"She's fine," Michael assured him quickly. "She, uh…she, um—" this wasn't going well "—she's just fine."

Michael could feel Joe Stanton waiting on the other end of the line. "Your sister's been working for me, Joe. She's been taking care of my daughter, Hailey."

"Yes. She mentioned that." Suspicion coated every word.

It was nothing but pure anxiety that had Michael blurting, "She's driving me nuts."

The comment was met with dead silence. Not a good thing to say, he decided immediately, but he plowed ahead. "I probably shouldn't be calling you. But I don't know what else to do. I've fallen for her, Joe. I know it's only been a few weeks. But stranger things have happened, you've got to admit. I'm in love with the woman. And I know she feels it, too." He frowned. "Or at least I know she feels something. But she's being stubborn. She's refusing to even explore the possibilities. And I'm at my wit's end here. And I certainly don't want to push her into going on a date when she's so dead set against it. But I'm afraid she—*we*—might be passing up something good. Something special."

Never in his life had he used so many conjunctions while trying to convey his thoughts. He gripped the phone receiver so tightly that his hand began to ache. He wished Joe Stanton would say something. Call him an idiot. Demand that he stay away from his sister. Threaten to call the police. Any verbal response would be better than this interminable silence.

Sophia's brother exhaled. "Is she giving you that 'blazing course' crap?"

Every muscle in Michael's body loosened and his head felt light with relief. Maybe this would turn out to be a productive conversation after all.

As Monday mornings went, this one was quite uneventful. Undoubtedly, Karen had become proficient at running the office, of anticipating problems before they arose and fixing those she was unable to thwart. Sophia regretted not hiring her full-time before now.

With no messes to straighten out, though, Sophia felt at loose ends. At least when she was working for Michael, she'd had Hailey to tend to.

She smiled, thinking of the sweet, dark-eyed, tawny-haired baby. Closing her eyes, she could almost smell the soft, warm scent of baby powder. An odd longing squeezed at her. But another imaginary fragrance soon encroached on her thoughts; a heated, masculine aroma that made her heart trip across its regular rhythm.

Michael.

Shoving him from her thoughts, she snatched some forms off her desk, rose from her chair and went to the file cabinet. Keeping her hands and her mind busy was the only way she was going to forget him. And forgetting him was the only way she could get her life back in order.

She wished she could shake this forlorn feeling. It made no sense. She'd set a goal for herself, and she was following it to the T. She should be pleased that everything worked out well with Michael and Hailey. Fay would be the perfect nanny for them. And Sophia was free to get back to managing her business.

The file cabinet drawer closed with a clunk and she paused a moment to press her hand to her diaphragm, willing away the strange gloom that was lumped there.

Karen rapped on her door twice and then pushed it open without waiting for an invitation.

Her eyes were round and words tumbled off her tongue. "He's here. Again. Mr. Taylor. He just pulled up out front." She gave a little gasp. "He parked in the fire lane, Sophia!"

Just seconds later, the bells on the front door announced his arrival.

Thin burgundy pinstripes shot through the charcoal fabric of his suit. The cut of his jacket accentuated his broad build. Sophia forced her gaze to lift to his face.

"Morning," he greeted both Karen and Sophia.

Karen's smile looked as fake as a three-dollar bill. "Coffee, tea?" she offered.

"No, thanks." His gaze swung to Sophia. "I need a few minutes of your time."

That's the Michael she knew, demanding and authoritative.

"If you don't mind," he added.

She blinked. The query softening his tone was a surprise. Determined not to be thrown, Sophia glanced at her wristwatch.

"Fay was due to arrive at eight. She's never been late in all the years she's worked as a nanny, so I know that can't be the problem." She rested her arm on top of the file cabinet. "You couldn't have spent more than an hour and a half getting to know the woman. So, for the life of me, I can't figure out what you could possibly have to complain about."

He looked perplexed. "I'm not here to complain about Mrs. Richardson. She's perfect. She's everything I ever wanted in a nanny."

Now it was Sophia's turn to look confused. "Okay, then what *are* you here to complain about?"

He placed his hand over his heart. "Sophia, you wound me. You talk as if I'm a big bellyacher."

She refused to smile, asking pointedly, "When have you come to my office and not caused a problem?"

"Touché." He slipped his hands into his pockets. "I didn't come here to cause problems for you, Sophia."

His sincerity was captivating. Did he have to be so handsome, so darn charming? She wanted to look away, but didn't dare. She had to remain vigilant against him and the feelings he instilled in her.

"I came here to solve some."

Truly bewildered, she leaned a little heavier on the cabinet, waiting, certain he intended to expound.

"Oh, before I forget." He reached into the breast pocket located on the inside of his jacket and pulled out a white envelope. "You left this at my place Saturday night."

She stepped forward, accepted it and then moved back next to the file cabinet. "You could have mailed this."

An intense aura seemed to buzz all around him as he told her, "I needed to see you, Sophia."

She studied his face, searching her chaotic thoughts for an appropriate response. Her voice grated when she finally replied, "Michael, I've already told you—"

"I know what you told me." Again, he stuffed his hands into his pockets. "That you've made plans for your life that don't include a man, or a relationship. You're focusing on your career." He nodded. "I understand." Almost to himself, he added, "I understand *a lot* now."

Thinking back to Saturday night when she'd rejected his advances, Sophia realized that she hadn't mentioned her decision to focus on her career. She'd only told him she'd made some choices. But, being an intelligent man, he'd obviously put a few things together.

"You obviously have some reservations about intimate relationships. Viable reservations that were validated by your rough childhood."

A frown pinched her face. How much of her past had she revealed to him during the three weeks she lived in his home?

"You made a comment last week that intrigued me," he continued. "You talked about being strict with your brother. I thought it odd at the time…that you were somehow inferring that you were the disciplinarian in your brother's life. I've discovered that you were just that."

Her frown deepened. Being astute was one thing, but he seemed to be privy—and way too sure—about particulars that he should know nothing about.

"Your father left before you hit your teens." Deep compassion etched his face. "Your mother was forced to work two and sometimes three jobs to make ends meet. Which left you the overwhelming responsibilities of taking care of the house and raising your brother."

"Now, hold on," she protested. "Wait just one darn second. I don't remember telling you all those details."

He nodded. "You didn't. Your brother did."

"You talked to Joe? When? Why? I don't understand."

"Please don't be upset with him. I got myself in a state yesterday, pretty desperate for some information when I called him. I was afraid he'd think I was some weirdo, calling him out of the blue like that. But I shot straight with him. Poured my heart out, really. And he was good about it."

Shot straight? Poured his heart out?

Hesitancy colored his tone when he softly said, "I told him that I love you, Sophia."

Conflicting emotion barraged her, swirled around in her head…and her heart. But sheer panic made her break out in a sweat.

"I can't do this, Michael." She stood rod-straight. "I can't."

He ignored her. "You feel something for me, Sophia. I know you do. And it's unfair to both of us if you ignore what you're feeling."

Needing some kind of shield, some kind of barrier between them, she stalked to her desk and fled to the far side…the safe side.

"*I have a plan.*" The harshness with which she spit out the words didn't affect him in the least.

"And you can continue with it." He shrugged. "Lots of married women have careers. Most of them do these days."

Married? Her panic metamorphosed into stark, raving fear.

"Marriage is for fools. Marriage doesn't last." Her

heart cracked liked fragile glass when she said, "My father taught me that men don't stay."

Michael approached the desk. "And my father taught me that they do."

In that instant, it seemed that the sun broke above the horizon to brighten, what had been for her, a very dark night.

Sylvia and Bradley Taylor shared a happy and loving marriage. They'd been wonderful parents, and Bradley had to have been a good father—an available father—who had taught his son well. Why else would Michael have felt so strongly about taking responsibility for Hailey? There were other choices he could have made in that situation, but he hadn't made them. He'd held himself to a higher standard. Made himself accountable for his actions.

A man like that could very well change her perceptions of life.

She was seized by a swelter that left her breathless and teary-eyed. "I'm afraid," she whispered.

He smiled, a short exhalation leaving him in a rush. "I'm scared, too. That's got to be a normal reaction when you're embarking on something new." Slowly but surely, he made his way around the desk. "But, Sophia, I'm also excited and happy and amazingly hopeful."

Uncertainty had her heart pounding, and he must have sensed what she was feeling.

"Please stop focusing on the past," he said, opening his arms to her. "Didn't you tell me that it's not the past that matters? What matters is the present and the future and what you do with them. What *we* do with them, Sophia."

She stared at him, love and hope slowly filtering through the haze of her fear.

"You don't have to go it alone. We'll have each other."
He grinned. "And let's not forget Mrs. Richardson."

To have a gaggle of children to love, a man who was willing to be there, eager to share the duties of hearth and home. Before this moment, those things seemed like impossibilities. But he helped her to believe that she really could have it all; a satisfying career, a loving family and a devoted man to adore.

Joy and anticipation chased away every shadowy doubt when she stepped into his arms. Cupping his face between her hands, she pulled him to her and kissed him fiercely.

His arms wrapped around her, hugging her tight as if he had found a long lost treasure that he didn't intend to lose again. She closed her eyes, reveling in the shelter of his love.

"I have a message from Joe." His mouth was a hair's breath from her ear. Without loosening his hold on her one iota, he said, "He's been having lunch with a woman. The music teacher at his school. He was hoping you'd break the pact so that he could ask her out on a date."

Sophia gasped, but then she laughed and squeezed Michael tighter. She wove her fingers into his silky hair. "Wait'll I see that rat fink. He's in a heap of trouble."

Michael pulled back, humor sparking in his eyes. Or was that desire?

"Be gentle. I owe your brother a great deal."

Completely understanding his meaning, she said, "So do I."

Their kiss was interrupted by a sharp rap on the door. Total disbelief registered on Karen's face when she stepped into the office and witnessed their cozy embrace.

"There's a police officer out front." The young woman was clearly flustered. "He's ticketing your vehicle,

Mr. Taylor. I went out there, but there was no talking him out of it."

Michael tipped back his head and laughed. "That's okay. I was in such a hurry to get in here, I parked in the fire lane. I have to take responsibility for my actions." He gazed lovingly into Sophia's face. "I don't mind paying the ticket. This is worth every dollar."

* * * * *

The next book in
THE BRIDES OF BELLA LUCIA *series*
is out next month!
Don't miss THE REBEL PRINCE
by Raye Morgan
Here's an exclusive sneak preview of
Emma Valentine's story!

"OH, NO!"

The reaction slipped out before Emma Valentine could stop it, for there stood the very man she most wanted to avoid seeing again.

He didn't look any happier to see her.

"Well, come on, get on board," he said gruffly. "I won't bite." One eyebrow rose. "Though I might nibble a little," he added, mostly to amuse himself.

But she wasn't paying any attention to what he was saying. She was staring at him, taking in the royal blue uniform he was wearing, with gold braid and glistening badges decorating the sleeves, epaulettes and an upright collar. Ribbons and medals covered the breast of the short, fitted jacket. A gold-encrusted sabre hung at his side. And suddenly it was clear to her who this man really was.

She gulped wordlessly. Reaching out, he took her

elbow and pulled her aboard. The doors slid closed. And finally she found her tongue.

"You...you're the prince."

He nodded, barely glancing at her. "Yes. Of course."

She raised a hand and covered her mouth for a moment. "I should have known."

"Of course you should have. I don't know why you didn't." He punched the ground-floor button to get the elevator moving again, then turned to look down at her. "A relatively bright five-year-old child would have tumbled to the truth right away."

Her shock faded as her indignation at his tone asserted itself. He might be the prince, but he was still just as annoying as he had been earlier that day.

"A relatively bright five-year-old child without a bump on the head from a badly thrown water polo ball, maybe," she said defensively. She wasn't feeling woozy any longer and she wasn't about to let him bully her, no matter how royal he was. "I was unconscious half the time."

"And just clueless the other half, I guess," he said, looking bemused.

The arrogance of the man was really galling.

"I suppose you think your 'royalness' is so obvious it sort of shimmers around you for all to see?" she challenged. "Or better yet, oozes from your pores like...like sweat on a hot day?"

"Something like that," he acknowledged calmly. "Most people tumble to it pretty quickly. In fact, it's hard to hide even when I want to avoid dealing with it."

"Poor baby," she said, still resenting his manner. "I guess that works better with injured people who are half asleep." Looking at him, she felt a strange emotion she couldn't identify. It was as though she wanted to prove something to him, but she wasn't sure what. "And anyway, you know you did your best to fool me," she added.

His brows knit together as though he really didn't know what she was talking about. "I didn't do a thing."

"You told me your name was Monty."

"It is." He shrugged. "I have a lot of names. Some of them are too rude to be spoken to my face, I'm sure." He glanced at her sideways, his hand on the hilt of his sabre. "Perhaps you're contemplating one of those right now."

You bet I am.

That was what she would like to say. But it suddenly occurred to her that she was supposed to be working for this man. If she wanted to keep the job of coronation chef, maybe she'd better keep her opinions to herself. So she clamped her mouth shut, took a deep breath and looked away, trying hard to calm down.

The elevator ground to a halt and the doors slid open laboriously. She moved to step forward, hoping to make her escape, but his hand shot out again and caught her elbow.

"Wait a minute. *You're* a woman," he said, as though that thought had just presented itself to him.

"That's a rare ability for insight you have there, Your Highness," she snapped before she could stop herself. And then she winced. She was going to have to do better than that if she was going to keep this relationship on an even keel.

But he was ignoring her dig. Nodding, he stared at her with a speculative gleam in his golden eyes. "I've been looking for a woman, but you'll do."

She blanched, stiffening. "I'll do for what?"

He made a head gesture in a direction she knew was

opposite of where she was going and his grip tightened on her elbow.

"Come with me," he said abruptly, making it an order.

She dug in her heels, thinking fast. She didn't much like orders. "Wait! I can't. I have to get to the kitchen."

"Not yet. I need you."

"You what?" Her breathless gasp of surprise was soft, but she knew he'd heard it.

"I need you," he said firmly. "Oh, don't look so shocked. I'm not planning to throw you into the hay and have my way with you. I need you for something a bit more mundane than that."

She felt color rushing into her cheeks and she silently begged it to stop. Here she was, formless and stodgy in her chef's whites. No makeup, no stiletto heels. Hardly the picture of the femmes fatales he was undoubtedly used to. The likelihood that he would have any carnal interest in her was remote at best. To have him think she was hysterically defending her virtue was humiliating.

"Well, what if I don't want to go with you?" she said in hopes of deflecting his attention from her blush.

"Too bad."

"What?"

Amusement sparkled in his eyes. He was certainly enjoying this. And that only made her more determined to resist him.

"I'm the prince, remember? And we're in the castle. My orders take precedence. It's that old pesky divine rights thing."

Her jaw jutted out. Despite her embarrassment, she couldn't let that pass.

"Over my free will? Never!"

Exasperation filled his face.

"Hey, call out the historians. Someone will write a book about you and your courageous principles." His eyes glittered sardonically. "But in the meantime, Emma Valentine, you're coming with me."

SAVE UP TO $30! SIGN UP TODAY!

INSIDE *Romance*

The complete guide to your favorite Harlequin®, Silhouette® and Love Inspired® books.

✓ Newsletter ABSOLUTELY FREE! No purchase necessary.

✓ Valuable coupons for future purchases of Harlequin, Silhouette and Love Inspired books in every issue!

✓ Special excerpts & previews in each issue. Learn about all the hottest titles before they arrive in stores.

✓ No hassle—mailed directly to your door!

✓ Comes complete with a handy shopping checklist so you won't miss out on any titles.

- -

SIGN ME UP TO RECEIVE INSIDE ROMANCE ABSOLUTELY FREE
(Please print clearly)

Name _____

Address _____

City/Town _____ State/Province _____ Zip/Postal Code _____

(098 KKM EJL9)

Please mail this form to:
In the U.S.A.: Inside Romance, P.O. Box 9057, Buffalo, NY 14269-9057
In Canada: Inside Romance, P.O. Box 622, Fort Erie, ON L2A 5X3
OR visit http://www.eHarlequin.com/insideromance

IRNBPA06R   ® and ™ are trademarks owned and used by the trademark owner and/or its licensee.

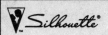

Page-turning drama...

Exotic, glamorous locations...

Intense emotion and passionate seduction...

Sheikhs, princes and billionaire tycoons...

This summer, may we suggest:

THE SHEIKH'S DISOBEDIENT BRIDE
by Jane Porter
On sale June.

AT THE GREEK TYCOON'S BIDDING
by Cathy Williams
On sale July.

THE ITALIAN MILLIONAIRE'S VIRGIN WIFE
On sale August.

With new titles to choose from every month,
discover a world of romance in our books written
by internationally bestselling authors.

SILHOUETTE *Romance*

COMING NEXT MONTH

#1830 THE RANCHER TAKES A FAMILY—Judy Christenberry
Widowed rancher John Richey had sworn off women, but he would
do anything for his baby daughter—even remarry to give her a
mother. Debra Williams seemed the ideal choice for a marriage in
name only. Until she and her toddler son moved in and made his
house feel like a home again....

#1831 WINNING BACK HIS BRIDE—Teresa Southwick
Wealthy businessman Michael Sullivan needs advice on the most
important project of his career, and only one woman can help him—
Geneva Porter. But what man would want to work with the woman
who had left him standing at the altar? And could Michael still have
a vacancy for her...as his bride?

#1832 THE CINDERELLA FACTOR—Sophie Weston
The French château is the perfect hiding place for Jo—until its
owner, sardonic reporter Patrick Burns, comes home.... Patrick
thinks the secret runaway is a thief until he sees that Jo is hiding a
painful past. But as his feelings for her grow, can he prove to be her
Prince Charming?

#1833 THE BOSS'S CONVENIENT BRIDE—Jennie Adams
Claire Dalgliesh is stunned when her boss declares that he needs
a wife—and he's selected her for the job! Claire may have a huge
crush on Nicholas Monroe, but she's not going to walk up the aisle
with him—not without love. At least, that's what she thinks....